STACEY McGILL . . .
MATCHMAKER?

Other books by
Ann M. Martin

P.S. Longer Letter Later
(written with Paula Danziger)
Leo the Magnificat
Rachel Parker, Kindergarten Show-off
Eleven Kids, One Summer
Ma and Pa Dracula
Yours Turly, Shirley
Ten Kids, No Pets
Slam Book
Just a Summer Romance
Missing Since Monday
With You and Without You
Me and Katie (the Pest)
Stage Fright
Inside Out
Bummer Summer

THE KIDS IN MS. COLMAN'S CLASS series
BABY-SITTERS LITTLE SISTER series
THE BABY-SITTERS CLUB mysteries
THE BABY-SITTERS CLUB series
CALIFORNIA DIARIES series

STACEY McGILL . . . MATCHMAKER?

Ann M. Martin

AN
APPLE
PAPERBACK

SCHOLASTIC INC.
New York Toronto London Auckland Sydney
Mexico City New Delhi Hong Kong

Dedicated to Ren Roome
and Ann Ross Roome.

Cover art by Hodges Soileau

ISBN 0-590-50175-5

12 11 10 9 8 7 6 5 4 3 2 8 9/9 0 1 2 3/0

Printed in the U.S.A. 40

First Scholastic printing, November 1998

The author gratefully acknowledges
Suzanne Weyn
for her help in
preparing this manuscript.

I closed my book and drummed my fingers on its cover. *Pride and Prejudice* by Jane Austen. I'd groaned when Mom suggested reading it together. After all, how exciting could the lives of prim, proper people in the 1800s be? But to my surprise it was much more interesting than I'd expected.

"I'm almost ready, Stacey," Mom called into the living room, where I sat. She was across the hall in the dining room, pulling out our good dishes from the hutch and laying them on the table for inspection. This is something she does every year before Thanksgiving.

I'd asked Mom for a few extra minutes so I could finish the chapter I was reading. You see, we'd agreed to start a mother-daughter reading group. The idea was, we'd pick a book and then both read it. Each week we'd sit together and discuss the chapters we'd read.

When I'd finished reading, I walked to the

dining room. "Mom, what exactly are we doing for Thanksgiving dinner this year?" I asked.

She looked up blankly from the dish she'd been inspecting. I noticed a hairline crack across the middle. "I'm sorry, what did you say?" she asked.

"Thanksgiving," I repeated. "What are we doing?"

"I'm not sure," she admitted. Before Mom and Dad were divorced, they always invited friends to dinner. (Most of our family lives too far away to visit.) But since the divorce, Mom has pretty much drifted away from the couples she and Dad used to hang out with. Besides, most of them are in New York City, where Dad still lives. But Mom and I live in Stoneybrook, Connecticut. Although it's less than two hours from the city, it feels farther away. That may be because it's so quiet and suburban — so completely different from the city. It's enough of a distance to make us both lose track of most of our old friends.

I have two advantages over Mom, though. The first major plus is that I've made amazing new friends. We're all part of a group called the Baby-sitters Club. (I'll tell you more about that later.)

Second, I still travel to the city on a regular basis to visit Dad. You could say I lead a double life. I'm part suburban Stoneybrooker and part city girl. My boyfriend, Ethan, lives in the city too, so I have lots of reasons to want to get into New York as much as I can.

Mom, though, almost never goes into the city. She's too busy with her job as a buyer for Bellair's Department Store, which is here in Stoneybrook. (A buyer is someone who selects the things the store is going to sell to its customers.) She says there's no reason for her to go to the city, except when she has to go to Manhattan for work.

I argue that there are museums, plays, movies — a zillion other reasons for her to go. She just shrugs and says everything comes to Stamford eventually. (Stamford is the city closest to Stoneybrook.) I always shriek, "Stamford! How can you compare Stamford to New York City?" No offense to Stamford, but it is *not* an international center of culture and business like Manhattan.

Mom laughs and says she spent her whole life in New York City, and now she's happy to live at a slower pace.

Okay, I can accept that. But what I don't understand is why she hasn't made many friends. "Adults don't make new friends the way young people do," she insists. "Besides, I'm too busy right now for new friendships."

That sounds like a pretty lame excuse. Yes, she's got a job, but she's not a workaholic like my dad. He's a lawyer and he lives and breathes his job. Mom doesn't do that — thank goodness. And it's not as if she has eight kids or something. There's only me.

Of course, it's none of my business. Mom can live her life any way she chooses. I just think she *must* be lonely. Who wouldn't be?

Mom hasn't had a single date since the divorce. My dad already has a new steady girlfriend, Samantha. I'm not eager for a stepdad, but it would be nice for Mom if she went out once in awhile.

Sure, she's got me, and we're extremely close. Closer, I think, than most mothers and daughters. But I'm thirteen. Doesn't she want adult friends too? I mean, I love her — totally — but I wouldn't want to spend *all* my free time with her.

"I'll think about Thanksgiving later," she said, putting down the cracked dish. "It's almost three weeks away, after all."

"Good idea," I agreed. "Let's talk about the book."

We went to the living room and sat on the couch. I plucked a carrot stick from a plate on the coffee table. It was my midafternoon snack. Mom waited patiently for me to finish it. She knows I can't let myself get hungry because I have a chronic (meaning, never-ending) condition called diabetes.

A diabetic can't properly regulate the amount of sugar in his or her bloodstream. This happens automatically for most people. In my case, I have to give myself daily injections of something called insulin. I also have to eat only healthy foods, no sweets or junk food. And, as I said, I can't skip meals or let myself get hungry.

Not paying attention to these things could be a majorly big deal. (I'm talking coma or even death.) But if I do what I'm supposed to do, it's not a problem. By now, it's become second nature for me to eat right and take my injections. I hardly even notice it.

When I'd finished munching, Mom sat forward on the couch. "So? What do you think of the book so far?" she asked.

"It's good," I admitted. "Elizabeth is pretty cool." Elizabeth Bennett is the main character and not at all what you'd expect from a young woman from that era. I thought she'd be prim and proper. But she's outspoken and witty, even mischievous, in a way.

"I think her independence shows that she's brave," Mom said. "When you consider how little opportunity there was for women in those days, it takes real guts to stand on her own the way she does."

"I know," I agreed. "You have to admire someone who would rather be poor than degrade herself by trying to snare a rich husband."

Mom nodded. "Especially when that was what all the other women around her were doing. It shows a lot of self-respect and pride."

"Maybe too much pride," I suggested as an idea came to me.

"What do you mean?" Mom asked.

"Well . . . she's so proud that she assumes Mr. Darcy is looking down on her because she's poor. But she doesn't really know that to be true. She snubs him before he can snub her. Isn't that reverse snobbery? Shouldn't she at least give him a chance?"

"You have a point," Mom said. "I can understand how she would feel defensive, though. Mr. Darcy is so wealthy. All the women are after him. She's not about to join the crowd."

"I'm glad I wasn't born back then," I said. "What if no one wanted to marry me? There would be nothing else for me to do."

"I don't think you would have to worry," Mom said with a smile. "You're intelligent and fun to be with. They'd all be bringing you flowers. You could take your pick."

I thought about my boyfriends. I'd already had a couple. I've told you about Ethan. Before him, I dated a guy named Robert. We had our problems, but we're friends now. Even before that I knew some boys who liked me.

A really icky thought came to me. "What if you had to pick your boyfriend based on how rich he was? Wouldn't that be horrible?"

"Some women do that even nowadays," Mom said.

"You're joking!"

"I'm afraid not. I personally know several women who say they would never even date a man unless he had lots of money."

"That's repulsive! Tell them to get their own money."

Mom smiled. "You're an independent spirit, like Elizabeth."

"Oh, well, give me credit for having a little self-respect," I said.

Mom patted my knee. "I give you credit for having tons of self-respect."

"You too," I said. "You didn't marry Dad because he was rich."

"He wasn't rich," Mom said. "He was a public defender when I met him." I knew that meant he had defended clients who couldn't pay for their own lawyer.

A faraway look came into her eyes. "I wonder if we would still be married if he'd stayed in that job."

"What do you mean?" I asked.

"Well, I respected the work of a public defender. I felt your dad was giving himself to something worthwhile. Once he became a corporate lawyer, negotiating deals and contracts, I didn't have as much regard for what he was doing. I started to resent all the time he spent at work."

"Wasn't that kind of judgmental of you?" I said cautiously, not wanting to hurt her feelings. "I mean, his job was his choice."

Mom smiled, but it was a sad, wistful smile. "Yes, it was."

I couldn't stand seeing her sad, so I changed the subject. "The clothes in the book are awesome. Don't you think?"

"Could you stand to wear a long skirt all the time?"

"I don't know, but it would be cool to get all dressed up every single day. It would be fun to swish around in a fancy dress."

Mom laughed. "I'd be afraid every time I turned around that I'd trip on the hem of my skirt."

"Yeah, there you are, trying to impress some millionaire and every time you move, you stumble over your skirt."

This made us both laugh. Which is the best thing about the reading group — that Mom and I can share something, even if it's only a joke.

"Stacey, are you free tomorrow?" Mary Anne Spier asked me. It was Monday, and I'd just stepped into Claudia Kishi's bedroom for a meeting of the Baby-sitters Club.

My eyes darted to the clock on Claudia's desk. Was I late? It read 5:27. So I was actually a full three minutes early. The BSC (which is what we call the Baby-sitters Club) meets every Monday, Wednesday, and Friday afternoon at five-thirty sharp. Our clients can call us until six to line up a baby-sitter.

"Did someone call before the meeting started?" I asked. All our regular customers know better than to do that.

"I didn't even want Claudia to pick up the phone," Kristy Thomas said.

Claudia rolled her eyes. "Excuse me, but it could have been for me. This *is* my room and my phone."

"The rule is five-thirty to six," Kristy insisted. "Otherwise you'll go crazy answering the phone every minute. The rule is for your sake."

"Don't argue," Mary Anne pleaded. "The fact is, Claudia *did* answer it and now we have a job to fill."

"Who called?" I asked, settling in on Claudia's bed.

"A new customer, Mr. Brooke," Mary Anne told me. "He's never used us before, so I guess we can forgive him for calling early."

Mallory Pike spoke up from her usual spot on the floor. "He's an okay person."

"Mrs. Pike recommended us to him," Jessi Ramsey added, sitting cross-legged beside Mallory, who's her best friend.

"She met him at a parent-teacher conference the other night," Mallory explained. "His son is in Claire's kindergarten class." Claire is the youngest of Mallory's seven brothers and sisters. "She told him to call us if he needed a sitter."

"Only, no one but you is free tomorrow," Mary Anne told me as she looked down at the BSC record book, in which she keeps track of our sitting jobs.

Mary Anne also keeps track of our schedules in that book. For example, she knows when I'm going to see Dad. Or when I have a Math Club meeting. (I love math.) Or when anybody has a class or a meeting or an appointment. That helps make her the scheduling whiz she is. She's the club secretary and I can't imagine anyone doing a better job.

"Okay," I said. "I'll do it."

Since Claudia had taken the call, she'd written the details about the job on a yellow legal pad. That's how we operate. The person nearest the phone answers a call and takes down the name, day, time, address, and other facts about the job. Then she says she'll call the client back to tell him or her who the sitter will be. "You can call back Mr. Brooke and say I'll be there," I told Claudia.

"Excellent," Kristy said as Claudia punched in Mr. Brooke's number. Kristy is president of the club, which was her idea to begin with. "A new client! Yesss!"

I grinned. Kristy's skill at getting and keeping clients is what's made the BSC such a huge success. One of the things, anyway.

It's funny. Kristy is someone you could easily underestimate. She's petite, with long, medium brown hair and a plain, sporty style of dressing. If you looked at her you might not guess right away that she's a dynamo in a tiny simple package. She is, though. She's always coming up with great ideas for improving the club. She's an outspoken leader who gets things done.

Kristy is so down-to-earth you might not suspect she lives in a mansion. She didn't always, though. Most of her life she lived in an average kind of house. Her father abandoned her mother, her three brothers (two older, one younger), and Kristy when Kristy was seven. Mrs. Thomas had to struggle to raise her kids on her own. She did a good job of it. Eventually, she met Watson Brewer and married him.

Kristy's life certainly changed then. She and her family moved into Watson's mansion on the other — wealthier — side of town. She became a big sis to Watson's kids from his first marriage. Her stepsibs are Karen, who is seven, and Andrew, who is four. (They spend half the time with Watson and half with their mother and her new husband, in another part of Stoneybrook.) Watson and Kristy's mom also adopted a little girl from Vietnam named Emily Michelle, who is now about two and a half. Kristy's grandmother, Nannie, moved in to help out with Emily Michelle. So Kristy's family quickly became huge. Throughout these changes, she's somehow managed to remain completely herself — upbeat and in charge.

Before Kristy could get in another word, Abby Stevenson burst into the room, her long, dark curls flying behind her. "What did I miss? I know I'm late." She dropped to her knees in front of Kristy. "A thousand pardons, Madam President. I am exceedingly sorry."

Kristy half laughed and half frowned. "Anna called and told me you'd be a little late and that you wouldn't be driving over with Charlie and me," Kristy said, which was as much forgiveness as anyone could expect from her. Kristy despises it when we're even one minute late. In fact, Abby *was* only one minute late. It was 5:31.

With a dramatic flourish, Abby pretended to wipe her forehead in exaggerated relief.

"Why didn't you come home after school?" Kristy asked. Kristy, Abby, and Anna (Abby's twin) live in the same neighborhood. They usually get a ride to meetings from Kristy's older brother Charlie, since they live too far away to walk.

"Emergency soccer meeting," Abby reported as she sat on the bed. "Coach wants to know why we aren't winning."

"Well, why aren't you?" Kristy asked. Like Abby, Kristy is a serious athlete. She even coaches a kids' softball team called Kristy's Krushers.

"Because we have a couple of real dweebs on the team," Abby replied. "Anna could play better than they can."

That was saying a lot considering that Anna

isn't athletic at all. She's a talented violinist who's devoted to her music. She'd much rather play the national anthem than take a swing in the World Series.

There are other differences between Abby and Anna. For instance, it's easy to tell them apart since Anna's curly, dark hair is short. And, even though they both wear glasses, they chose different frames. When they wear their contact lenses, it's usually not on the same day.

Anna was recently diagnosed with scoliosis, which is a curvature of the spine. Because of it, she has to wear a brace under her clothing for the next few years. It took some time, but Anna's used to it by now. Abby also has slight scoliosis, but not bad enough to need the brace. Luckily, Anna doesn't have allergies and asthma like Abby does. Abby always carries her inhaler with her in case she has an asthma attack.

Still, Abby and Anna are close. Their mother is like my father, totally devoted to her job. She commutes to Manhattan every day and isn't home much. That means Anna and Abby rely on each other for company. Abby says that after their father died in a car crash (which was back when they lived on Long Island) she and Anna really depended on each other. They still do, even if it's less obvious now.

By the time Abby and Kristy had stopped

talking soccer, Claudia had hung up the phone. "Mr. Brooke says to come right after school," she told me. "He's near the school, on Kimball Street. He'll drive you home so you won't have to walk after dark."

"Mom can probably pick me up on her way home from work," I said.

Claudia nodded. "Anyone want a Mallomar?" she asked as she opened her bottom dresser drawer and withdrew a bag.

Claudia is my best friend and I know her better than anyone, but she still amazes me and cracks me up. She has packages of sugary and salty treats stashed all over her room. She has to hide them because her parents don't approve of junk food. And I can't say I blame them. But looking at her you'd never guess Claudia is the queen of junk food. Her long hair glistens, she's slim, her skin is flawless, and her dark eyes shine.

Opening a brown bag on top of her dresser, Claudia pulled out a clear plastic package. "Check this out," she said, handing it to me.

In three separate compartments were sliced carrots and a small container of ranch dressing. "Cool," I said. I read the dip ingredients, checking for corn syrup or fructose or any other sweeteners that might be a problem for me. I didn't see any. "These are neat."

"I thought so too," Claudia said. "And it

made Mom very happy. She thought I wanted them for myself."

Claudia is our vice-president, but her real job is hostess. It's not much effort for her since her room is always fully supplied with treats. But I appreciate that she also goes out of her way to have healthy snacks on hand for me.

"Did you make those?" I asked as I noticed something gold flash against Claudia's black hair.

She pushed back her hair to reveal a pair of long, shiny earrings dotted with small clay beads. Then she drew out a long beaded necklace, which had fallen beneath the bib of her tie-dyed overalls. (She'd dyed them herself.) She held the necklace out to give me a better look. "I made these beads last night," she explained. "I tried a new method of baking the polymer clay." The beads were gorgeous — swirling colors mixed with little specks of shiny beads.

That was Claudia, always experimenting, always searching for a way to do something even more creatively than she'd done it the time before. She is an artist.

Unfortunately, she lets her obsession with art drain her brainpower for school. Claudia was even sent back to seventh grade for awhile. Now that she's in eighth grade again, things are *much* improved, but still a bit rough. For one thing, her spelling remains atrocious. Her parents find this especially shocking since Claudia's sixteen-year-old sister, Janine, is a genuine genius who has aced every test she's ever taken.

Thinking about school troubles made me think of Mallory. "How's everything going?" I asked her.

Mallory grimaced. "I didn't exactly get rave reviews at the parent-teacher conferences," she replied.

"Your teachers always adore you!" Mary Anne cried.

"They think I've suddenly developed a *negative attitude* toward school," Mallory said. "And they're right."

"I know how *that* is," Claudia mumbled with her mouth full of Mallomar.

Claudia had been seemingly born with a bad attitude toward school. Mallory's troubles were recent, though. They had started when Stoneybrook Middle School (which we all attend) allowed some of the kids to teach classes for a week. Mallory, who loves writing and literature, had volunteered for the program, and it didn't go well for her at all, partly because Mallory is eleven and in sixth grade and she was assigned to an eighth-grade English class.

In my opinion, that wasn't fair. When a few of the eighth-graders saw a sixth-grader walk in, they were determined to demolish her. Who knows why? Some kids are just mean.

We all hoped that since Mallory is the oldest of eight kids, she might be able to deal with the chaos better than another sixth-grader could. Plus, she's a good student and a gifted writer. Unfortunately, she's not used to rowdy older kids.

I suppose Mallory was a target some of them couldn't resist. She was earnest and sincere. Some kids can't stand sincerity. They have to ridicule it.

And then there's her appearance. We love Mallory and think she's adorable, even though she hates her looks. She has reddish-brown hair, glasses, braces, and freckles. She knows she's not classically beautiful. I suspect that her lack of confidence about her looks might be something the eighth-graders noticed. It probably just made her seem even more unsure of herself and easier to pick on.

Kristy and Mary Anne were in that class and did the best they could to help, but it wasn't enough. Mary Anne said she went home and cried after one of the classes. (Mary Anne is sensitive and cries easily. Still, it must have been pretty bad.)

The worst part was that during one class the chalk flew out of Mallory's hand while she wrote on the board, and some kids started calling her Spaz Girl. The name stuck and spread around school. Mallory knows kids are *still* calling her Spaz Girl and it hurts her feelings. A lot. In fact, it (and everything else) seems to have made her hate school. I was worried about her. She was acting entirely unlike herself.

Jessi patted Mallory's shoulder. "It's just that stupid English class," she said. "It threw you off. By our next report card things will be cool again."

Mallory nodded grimly. "My parents say they'd better be."

"Are your mom and dad angry?" Abby asked.

"Not really. I think they're more worried. They want me to try harder, though."

"So try harder," Kristy said.

"I guess." Mallory shrugged.

"This is just a little setback," Jessi insisted. Jessi is so loyal. Not that I was surprised. She's a nice person in general. She's also an amazing ballerina. She takes lessons in Stamford and has already danced in some professional productions.

"I sat for the Rodowskys yesterday afternoon," Jessi went on. "I need the notebook." Since Mallory and Jessi are eleven, they only take afternoon jobs unless they're sitting for their own families. The rest of us are thirteen.

The club notebook is where we record everything that happens on our sitting jobs. No one but Mallory (our writer) likes to write in it, but Kristy insists. It's a great way to keep track of what's happening with our clients.

"I took the boys to that new ice-cream place," Jessi reported as she wrote. "We had one like it in Oakley. They have great ice cream."

Jessi's family moved to Stoneybrook from a town in New Jersey, after her father was transferred to Stamford by his company. It took some adjusting for Jessi, since her old town was much more integrated than Stoneybrook. At first, some little-minded bigmouths tried to make the Ramseys feel unwelcome because they're African-American. The rest of us knew how stupid the bigmouths were, and the Ramseys made lots of good friends here in Stoneybrook.

"Dues day," I announced. A wave of groans and grumbling filled the room. This is more of a tradition than a genuine complaint. Everyone knows that each Monday I collect dues. We use the money to pay part of Claudia's phone bill, which is only fair; to pay Charlie to drive Kristy and Abby to and from Claudia's; and, when we need to, to restock our Kid-Kits.

Each of us has a Kid-Kit. It's a box filled with fun things to bring on sitting jobs, such as art supplies, games, books, anything a kid might enjoy. We don't bring them on every job, but they're great to have.

I passed around my manila envelope and everyone put their money into it, but Mary Anne hesitated. "Stacey, is there anything extra in the fund?"

"Not really," I replied. "Why?"

"I got a letter from Dawn yesterday and she wrote that she was starting a movie club with her friends. They all go to a movie and then they discuss it. I was thinking that would be fun for us to do," Mary Anne explained.

"That's the same idea as the book club Mom and I have," I said, and I explained what we were doing.

It didn't surprise me that Dawn had started a movie club — or that she'd told Mary Anne about it. You see, they're stepsisters, even though Dawn lives in California. Here's how that happened: Dawn Schafer moved here with her mom and brother from California after her parents divorced. Mrs. Schafer had grown up in Stoneybrook and wanted to be near her parents, who still live here.

Dawn and Mary Anne quickly became friends. At first they didn't seem to have a lot in common. Dawn was outgoing and self-confident. Mary Anne was shy and unsure. Still, they were able to disregard appearances and were soon close friends. Mary Anne introduced Dawn to the rest of us. We liked her and invited her to join the club, which she did.

Then one day Mary Anne and Dawn discovered that Dawn's mom used to date Mary Anne's dad in high school. Both of them were now single, since Mary Anne's mother had died when Mary Anne was a baby. (Mary Anne's father was loving but way too strict.) Mary Anne and Dawn concocted a scheme to reunite their parents. Against all odds, it worked. Mary Anne and Dawn became stepsisters!

Mary Anne and her dad, Richard, moved into the old farmhouse Dawn and her mother lived in. Dawn's brother, Jeff, had gone back to California to live with their father. That left Mary Anne, Richard, Dawn, and Sharon (Dawn's mom) to try to become a family. As you might expect, there were problems in the beginning, but they became a happy family pretty quickly.

Dawn, though, couldn't get over the feeling that she didn't really belong in Stoneybrook. She had friends, but she missed the life she'd known in southern California. After several trips back and forth, she finally decided to move in with her dad, her brother, and her father's new wife. She still comes back to Stoneybrook on vacations and holidays. When she's here, she comes to meetings and takes sitting jobs, which is why we made her an honorary BSC member.

When Dawn left, we replaced her with Abby, who took over her role as alternate officer. That means she has to know a little about every club office in case someone has to miss a meeting. Dawn did a good job, and so does Abby.

Dawn's departure was difficult on Mary Anne. She had us, though. She and Kristy are especially close since they've been friends since they were little. And Mary Anne also has her boyfriend, Logan Bruno. He's a sweet guy who is also in the eighth grade at Stoneybrook Middle School (SMS for short).

Logan is an associate member of the BSC. He doesn't come to meetings, but we call on him when we have a job no one can fill. Our other associate member is Shannon Kilbourne. She's too busy with school activities to attend meetings. She takes an occasional sitting job, though.

When I finished telling everyone about the reading group Mom and I had formed, Kristy said, "Let's start one of those instead of a movie club."

"I just began a great book," Abby said. "It's called *Jacob Have I Loved*, by Katherine Paterson. I'm not very far into it. I'd wait for the rest of you to catch up."

"I love her books!" Mary Anne exclaimed. "I cried all through the last chapter of *The Great Gilly Hopkins*. It was wonderful."

"*Bridge to Terabithia* is great too," Jessi added.

We decided to begin reading *Jacob Have I Loved.* With my school reading, *Pride and Prejudice,* and the new book, I would have a lot of reading. But that was okay. It sounded stimulating. It wasn't like I had a lot on my mind.

At least, on Monday I didn't. But that would change the next day, when I met the Brookes. After Tuesday, I'd have a whole lot to think about.

After the meeting that afternoon, I stuck around Claudia's room. I was lying across her bed, leafing through a few of her most recent sketches, when the phone rang.

Claudia picked it up. "Hello?" I watched her brow wrinkle as she listened to the person on the other end. "Well, she's here. You can ask her yourself. Hold on." She handed me the phone.

"For me?" I whispered.

Claudia nodded and mouthed the name John Brooke.

"Hello?" I said.

"Hello. I was wondering if it would be all right with you if I'm in the house when you sit tomorrow," Mr. Brooke said. "It suddenly occurred to me that it might not be."

"You're going to be at home? Are you sure you need me?"

He laughed. "Oh, believe me, I need you, all

right. Desperately. I promise you, you won't even see me."

"Okay . . ." I agreed.

"Great. Then I'll see you after school, Lacey."

"Stacey," I corrected him. "Okay. 'Bye." I hung up the phone. "He's going to be there, but I won't see him," I told Claudia.

She frowned. "Really? Maybe he wants to spy on you to see what kind of baby-sitter you are before he leaves you alone with his kids."

"Ew, maybe. But he has a nice voice. It's friendly and warm."

The next day, after school, I found the Brooke house easily. With my backpack slung over my shoulder, I rang the bell.

The door opened and I stood facing this very good-looking man. He had lots of dark hair, just slightly long. And the most awesome, almost unnaturally green eyes. He wasn't exactly tall, but he wasn't short either. Medium sized. And with a great build, as if he worked out in a gym.

I stared at him for probably a moment too long. Then I realized I was staring and laughed nervously to cover up my embarrassment. "Hi, I'm Stacey."

He extended his hand. "John Brooke," he said as we shook hands.

I stepped into the house. I noticed it had slightly less furniture than most houses in the neighborhood. There was a couch and a large dresser with a TV on it. A big mirror hung on the wall behind the dresser. In the middle of the room, a Persian rug sat on a finished wood floor. It reminded me more of a city apartment than a suburban home.

"Kids!" Mr. Brooke shouted. He turned to me with a smile. "They're very excited about meeting you."

A nine-year-old girl soon appeared on the stairs leading to the second floor. She looked startlingly like her father, with her long chestnut hair, very green eyes, and a spray of freckles across her nose. Unlike her father, she was tall and willowy. "Hi," she said shyly from the stairs.

"Stacey, this is Joni," Mr. Brooke said.

"Hi, Joni," I said.

A boy of about five bounded down the stairs past Joni. He had the same sturdy build as his father but a completely different face — fair with large hazel eyes and wispy light brown hair. "I'm Ewan. Do you think that's a dumb name?"

I laughed. "No, it's a cool name."

He smiled. "Thanks. Joe Peters — that's a kid in my class — he says only geeks are named Ewan."

"Oh, what does he know?" I scoffed.

"Not much," Joni said as she came down the

stairs. "I saw Joe Peters. He's the geekiest kid in their whole class. He's just jealous of Ewan."

I liked that Joni supported her little brother.

"I'll be in that room over there on the right," Mr. Brooke told me, nodding toward a closed door. "That's my study."

"Dad's a writer," Joni added with obvious pride.

Wow! Interesting, I thought. "What do you write?" I asked.

"Horrible stuff," Joni answered gleefully, before Mr. Brooke had the chance. "People being killed. Murderers running away from the police and shooting more people."

"Detective novels," Mr. Brooke amended. "And if I don't finish this one in a month, my editor will have a fit. That's why I need you to watch these guys, Stacey. So I can write. I tried to write only while they were in school, but it turns out that wasn't enough time. I'm incredibly behind right now."

"He's always late," Ewan offered with a smile.

Mr. Brooke scowled at him, but his eyes shone with laughter. "That's right, Ewan, rat me out. Tell on your old dad."

"It's true," Ewan insisted. "You're always saying it yourself. This is you." He clutched his hair with two pudgy hands and paced back and forth, crying, "I'm so behind schedule!

This will never get done. I'll have to give back the money. But I can't! I've already spent it!"

"Ewan!" Mr. Brooke tried to scold his son but burst into laughter instead. "Is that really how I sound?"

Joni grabbed her hair and joined in. "No one will ever give me a book contract again if I miss this deadline!" she exclaimed. "I'll have to go work in a fast-food place. That might be good. Then I could write a great novel at night — without all this deadline pressure."

Mr. Brooke cracked up. I didn't know if it would be polite to laugh, but I couldn't help smiling. The kids were pretty funny and Mr. Brooke's laughter was contagious.

"Okay, you guys, quit showing off," he said as he caught his breath. "You're making me look like a stressed-out lunatic."

"You're not," Joni said, patting his shoulder fondly. "You're a great writer."

Mr. Brooke smiled at her. "That's my girl." He got up from the couch. "Great writer or not, I have to get this book finished." He took a few steps toward his study. "In an emergency, you know where I am," he said to me. "But I'd really like you to think that I'm not here. Joni, you can show Stacey where everything is. Okay?"

"Okay, Dad," she replied.

"Is there anything you'd like to do?" I asked

the kids once Mr. Brooke had disappeared into his study.

"My grandma just sent Joni and me the video of *The Indian in the Cupboard,*" Ewan volunteered. He picked up the video from the couch. It was still half covered in mailing paper.

"I saw it at the movies, but I'd like to see it again," said Joni.

I'd read the book by Lynn Reid Banks and had loved the story, but I'd never seen the movie. I glanced at the TV. There wasn't any VCR. "It's connected to the downstairs TV," Joni said, reading my expression. "We have to use that one while Dad's working, anyway."

She led the way through a doorway off the kitchen and down a set of stairs to a finished basement. Ewan ripped the cellophane off the video and popped the tape into the VCR.

As we sat on a comfy, worn couch and watched the opening advertisements, I noticed a picture on top of the TV. It showed Mr. Brooke, the kids, and a gorgeous woman with rich chestnut curls. Mrs. Brooke, I assumed.

"That's my mom," Joni said, looking at me. "She's in Atlanta now. She's going to be on TV there, talking to people in the morning."

"Wow," I said, impressed. This was some family — a novelist and a TV personality. "Are you all going to move down there?"

"No, Mom doesn't want us there," Ewan offered sadly.

Joni punched his knee sharply. "Don't say that. She's very busy working on her new show right now and she wouldn't have time for us." She turned to me. "Mom and Dad just got divorced. Their divorce papers say we live with Dad but Mom can see us whenever she wants. She used to be a model."

"I can see she's very beautiful," I commented.

"Yes, she is," Joni agreed. "She says she's too old to be a model anymore so now she's going to be a famous TV star. She was offered this job in Atlanta, so she took it."

The movie had started and we fell silent watching it. I enjoyed it, but from time to time I found myself glancing at the picture on top of the TV. I wondered how Mrs. Brooke could stand to leave her kids behind. And then I thought about all the parents, like my own father, who live apart from their kids. With that in mind, I decided not to judge.

I became interested in the movie, and the time flew by. It had just ended when the doorbell rang. I ran up the stairs to answer it and almost ran into Mr. Brooke as he came out of his study. "Whoa, sorry," he apologized, stepping around me to get to the door.

It was Mom. She'd come to pick me up on her way home from work. "Hi, I'm Maureen McGill, Stacey's mother. Am I too early?" she asked, stepping into the living room.

Mr. Brooke introduced himself and offered his hand to Mom. "No, it's good you stopped me. Once I start writing, I could keep going for hours. Especially when I have a killer deadline."

"You're a writer," Mom noted, sounding impressed.

"Yeah, I'm afraid so," he replied with a smile. He turned toward a low bookcase by the door. "These are mine."

Mom's eyes widened slightly. "You're J. B. Angel!"

I leaned forward and saw that every book on the shelf was written by the same author, J. B. Angel.

Mr. Brooke chuckled. "When I was a deejay at my college radio station I called myself Johnny Angel. So when I became an author, I kept the pseudonym."

"Why don't you use your own name?" I asked.

"This way I can write about all sorts of bizarre crimes and criminals without having people hide from me at parties and school conferences."

"Gee, I never thought of that," I said.

"Did the kids drive you crazy?" he asked me.

"No, they were great." Joni and Ewan came into the room. They smiled at me gratefully. "It's true," I said to them.

Mom had taken one of the books off the shelf. "I loved this one," she said.

"You've read it?" Mr. Brooke asked, sounding surprised and pleased.

"Of course. I've read several of your books. I've really enjoyed them, though I have to say I didn't always sleep well at night after I finished them."

Mr. Brooke laughed. "I get many angry letters from husbands and wives who say their spouses keep the light on at night after they read my books."

"Oh, I was already divorced by the time I discovered your books, so my husband wouldn't have complained to you," Mom said as she perused the back cover of another book. "I haven't read this one."

"Take it," Mr. Brooke said. "Please."

She smiled at him. "Really?"

"Yeah, I have boxes of them." He smiled at her. "So, you're divorced?"

Mom nodded.

"Me too."

"Oh?" Something about the way Mom said that made me take notice. As if his being divorced were incredibly interesting news.

I studied Mom closely. Could she actually be . . . was it possible . . . *interested* in Mr. Brooke?

Claudia clutched her arms and shivered. "I tried to read one of J. B. Angel's books once." That didn't surprise me, since Claudia is a big mystery fan. She adores Nancy Drew books. "I couldn't finish it," she added. "It was too scary. Is he creepy?"

We were in her room for our regular Wednesday meeting. I was filling everyone in on our newest client.

"Not at all," I told her. "He's really nice. And guess what? I think my mother likes him."

"You mean *likes* likes him?" Abby asked.

I nodded just as the phone rang. I was the closest to it, so I answered. "Hello, Baby-sitters Club."

"Hello, this is John Brooke."

"Hi, Mr. Brooke, it's Stacey."

"Oh, hi, Stacey! Listen, are you free to sit tomorrow night? Maybe from six-thirty until about nine-thirty?"

"I can't definitely take the job until I talk to the other baby-sitters," I told him. "But I'll get back to you in a few minutes." That's how the club works. Clients aren't allowed to request a specific sitter. We share the work equally. I hung up and told Mary Anne the information. "I'm free, but if someone else wants the job, that's fine," I said.

No one spoke up. "The job's yours," Mary Anne said.

"What did you think of Mr. Brooke?" Mom asked Thursday evening as we ate supper together.

"Nice," I said. "And cute." I'd been waiting for her to ask me.

Mom nodded. "It's so amazing to actually meet J. B. Angel. I'll drive you over there this evening," she offered.

"I can ride my bike," I said.

"Absolutely not. You'd have to ride home after dark. It's better if I drive you."

"Okay," I agreed. She seemed awfully eager to drive over there.

By six-thirty, when we pulled up in front of the Brookes' house, it was dark. The front lamppost lit up the walkway. Mr. Brooke was outside with a golden retriever on a leash. I hadn't seen the dog on Tuesday. Mom climbed out of the car and walked around to talk to him. "She's my neighbors' dog," he explained as we approached. "I'm walking and feeding her while they're away."

"That's nice of you," Mom commented.

"Just being neighborly," he said casually. "You know, I'm sorry. I could have picked Stacey up. I should have thought to offer."

"No problem," Mom said. "I was on my way out anyway."

You liar! I thought, smiling to myself. It was the kind of lie I might tell a guy I liked if I walked past his locker to see him. *Oh, I have class just down the hall*, or something like that. Anything to make it seem as if I wasn't haunting the hallway in the hope of catching a glimpse of him.

I laughed to myself. That was exactly what Mom had just done.

"Are the kids inside?" I asked Mr. Brooke.

"Yes, and they're dying to see you," he answered. "Why don't you go in?"

"Okay. 'Bye, Mom!" With a wave to her, I walked to the front door. As I pulled it open, I noticed she was planted right there, chatting with Mr. Brooke.

Okay! I thought. *This is good.*

The moment I opened the front door, I spotted Joni and Ewan at the front window, anxiously peering out. "Are you spying on my mother?" I asked with a laugh.

Joni turned her head toward me sharply. "What are they talking about?" she demanded.

"I don't know — this and that."

Joni pressed her nose to the glass, then turned away, her lips set in a grim line. "My father thinks your mother is pretty," she said sullenly. "He said so after she left Tuesday."

This was good news to me. Exciting news. He liked her too! But the dour expression on Joni's face kept me from smiling.

"She *is* pretty," Ewan said, turning away from the window.

Still scowling, Joni opened the front closet and yanked out her jacket. "Where are you going?" I asked.

"Out to get my father," she said. "He's supposed to be working. This is why he's always late. He can't get down to work. He has no self-discipline."

Her statements struck me as oddly grown-up. In a minute I understood why. "That's what Mom always used to say," Ewan told me. "She said it every single day."

"She did not!" Joni barked at him. "And if she did, it was because she was right. She used to make him work, and since she's not here, that's my job now."

"Wait," I said. I didn't want Joni to wreck our parents' conversation. "Give them just a few more minutes."

She didn't take her hand off the doorknob.

"Do you have homework?" I asked her.

She nodded, wrinkling her nose. "My worst subject, math."

"That's my best subject. Want some help?"

I could see the battle raging in her head. She was torn between dragging her father to work or getting math out of the way. "I could use some help," she admitted. "But if he's not in here soon, I'm going to go get him."

"Okay," I agreed, "let's see that homework." Her backpack was on the couch. She pulled her math workbook from it and we sat down together while Ewan stretched out on the love seat and opened an easy-reader book called *The Wrong-Way Rabbit*.

Joni's fourth-grade class was working on number rounding and estimation. It was easy stuff for me, but Joni didn't get it at all. "This make no sense," she fumed.

"Yes, it does," I insisted. "It's simple, really." We became involved with it. Another fifteen minutes passed. I was dying to know if Mom was still out there or if she'd left and Mr. Brooke had simply gone off to finish walking the dog.

Ewan left the couch and passed by the window. Joni's head snapped up from her work. "Take a look. Are they still out there?" she asked her brother.

Before Ewan could reply, Mr. Brooke walked through the front door. "Everything under control in here?" he asked me.

"Everything's fine," I said.

"Great. I'd better get to my writing." He opened the door to his study and was gone.

"You shouldn't worry about your father getting his work done," I told Joni gently. I didn't want her to think of herself as her dad's taskmaster. I pointed to his books on the shelf. "Look at all the books he's already written. Somehow he gets it done."

"He wrote those when my mother was here to make him write," Joni objected.

I didn't have an answer for that one. But somehow it didn't seem right that a nine-year-old should have to worry about it. "I'm sure he'll be fine. He's working now, isn't he? What's his study like?"

"Very cool," Joni replied. "I think he used to be cool a long time ago before he got married and had us. You sort of get that idea from him."

The sound of a clacking typewriter came from his studio. "See?" I said. "He's working." Then I frowned. "He uses a *typewriter*?" I asked. I thought all authors worked on word processors nowadays. At the very least, on an electric typewriter, which wouldn't make that kind of noise.

"Only when he's thinking," Joni explained. "When he has a good idea all worked out, he works on his computer."

The clacking kept up for a long time. I wondered if that meant the writing wasn't going well. Joni and I continued to grapple with her homework while Ewan watched TV downstairs. Finally, she grasped the idea, and I felt proud of myself for tutoring her successfully.

After that, we pulled out the Brookes' Monopoly game. Ewan had to be my partner because the game was too difficult for him. He seemed to enjoy moving our piece around the board, counting out the money, and putting down the buildings.

Joni played, but she was quiet. I wondered if she was just tired or still thinking about her father's work.

At eight o'clock, I asked, "What time do you guys go to bed?"

"Ewan goes to bed at seven. I go at eight-thirty," Joni answered.

"Seven!" I cried, tickling Ewan. "You little sneak. Why didn't you tell me?"

"I can't tell time," he said. We put away the game and went upstairs. Ewan was easy to settle down since he was already tired.

Joni was still wide awake. "Do you want me to read with you?" I asked.

"No. But could I read alone for awhile?"

"I could get my book and we could read up here together," I offered.

"No. If you don't mind, I'd rather read alone. That's what I'm used to."

"Okay," I agreed, feeling ever so slightly hurt. I had the feeling that something had changed since Tuesday. "Good night," I said at her bedroom door. "Don't stay up too late."

"I won't," she assured me, and I left. Downstairs, the clacking had stopped. I hoped it meant Mr. Brooke had moved to his computer.

I took out my copy of *Jacob Have I Loved.* The book had hooked me. It was the story of twin teenage girls told from the point of view of one twin, Louise, who thinks her sister, Caroline, is the favored one.

I became so engrossed in the story that only a few minutes seemed to pass before the doorbell rang. Mom had arrived to pick me up. "Mr. Brooke said he'd be done around nine-thirty," she explained.

Almost the moment she spoke, Mr. Brooke came out of his study. "Maureen, hello," he greeted her warmly. "Care for a cup of tea?"

"Well, if you're having one."

Mr. Brooke looked at me. "Stacey, how about you?" I knew he was just being polite.

"If no one minds, I'd love to finish this chapter while you have your tea," I said.

"A passionate reader," Mr. Brooke said.

"That's what I like to see. Sure, finish your chapter." I could tell he was glad I'd said no. Nothing personal —he just wanted to be alone with Mom.

They went into the kitchen and I returned to the couch and opened my book. Despite my interest in the story, I couldn't read it. I was too busy listening to their conversation, which was easy to hear.

It was mostly small talk. The amazing part was how well they were hitting it off. Each acted as if what the other had to say was fascinating, even though they were discussing some new town taxes coming up for a vote and whether or not Stoneybrook should put a traffic light at a certain corner.

Becoming a little bored, I went upstairs to check on Joni. She was asleep with her book beside her. She looked so young and sweet. I pulled her blanket up and shut off the light.

By the time I went downstairs again, the conversation between Mr. Brooke and Mom had become much more personal. "I know, divorce is so difficult," I heard Mom say. "Eventually, you'll all adjust, though. It just takes time."

I moved silently back to the couch, opened my book, and continued to eavesdrop.

"Listen, Maureen," Mr. Brooke said. "I need to ask you something. Do you like theater? In this case, bad theater?"

Mom laughed. "Well, not particularly. Not bad theater."

"Maybe I should put it another way," Mr. Brooke said. "Do you like theater that might, through some miracle, turn out not to be totally terrible?"

"It depends. What are you talking about?"

"This is the thing. Several years ago, I wrote a play, a mystery. Now a theater group in Stamford is going to perform it. I saw one rehearsal and it . . . wasn't great. But that was a month ago. There's a chance it might have improved."

"I'll bet it has."

"Opening night is this Saturday," Mr. Brooke went on. "I have to go, of course, since I'm the playwright. But I could use some moral support — a friend to hide behind — in case it's really a disaster. Would you possibly be free to go?"

I froze as I waited for Mom's reply.

"Absolutely," she said with delight in her voice. "I'd love to."

"Terrific!"

Yes! I cheered silently, closing my book. *Yes!*

Saturday

Stacey, I know you're happy your mom finally has a date. But when I sat for Joni and Ewan I met two seriously bent-out-of-shape kids. Joni disliked me right away just because I'm your friend.

I couldn't sit for Joni and Ewan the night of Mom's date because I'd made plans to visit Dad and Ethan in the city that day.

I'd told Kristy that Ewan and Joni were adorable, so she expected the job to be a snap. When she arrived, though, she found Ewan pouting and Joni snapping at him. Not exactly the picture I'd painted for her.

The next day, when she called me, Kristy agreed that Mr. Brooke was seriously cute. "I felt sorry for him, though," she reported. "He was really nervous and Joni kept telling him the sweater he was wearing looked terrible. He'd put on another, and she'd shoot that one down too."

"*Did* the sweaters look terrible?" I asked.

"No. He looked fine in each one. I'm pretty sure Joni was trying to make him late. Did you know this date with your mom was the first date he had since his divorce?"

"No," I admitted. "Wow. It was the first date for the kids then too."

I recalled how I felt when I first learned about Samantha, Dad's girlfriend. In the back of my mind I had been holding the far-fetched hope that someday Dad and Mom might get back together. Dad's having a new girlfriend smashed that dream. It made their divorce seem absolutely final.

Kristy told me that finally Mr. Brooke realized Joni was succeeding in making him late, and he dashed out (wearing a green sweater, which probably looked great with his eyes). The moment he left, Joni hurled a throw pillow at the door behind him. "Have a rotten time!" she shouted after him.

Ewan started crying.

Kristy gaped at them. "What's wrong?" she asked, amazed by this outburst.

"I don't want another mom," Joni exploded. "I have a beautiful mother. I don't need a new, ugly one."

Ewan sobbed even harder.

"Whoa," Kristy said. "Hold on. Mrs. McGill isn't ugly. And who says she's going to be your mother?"

"Dad likes her. He said she's pretty," Joni said.

"She *is* pretty," Ewan sobbed.

"Shut up!" Joni snapped at him. "She's not. Our mother is pretty."

Kristy didn't see any tissues for Ewan, so she took toilet paper from the small downstairs bathroom and wiped his nose. "Why are *you* upset?" she asked him gently.

He sniffed a few times before answering. "Joni says Dad is marrying Stacey's mom and she'll be our wicked stepmother like in *Cinderella* and *Hansel and Gretel.*"

"And we'll never see our own, true mother again," Joni chimed in.

"Who told you these things?" Kristy asked.

"No one. I just know," Joni said.

"Sit down a minute, both of you," Kristy said. With her arm around Ewan, she walked to the couch. Joni sat on the love seat. "I have a stepfather," Kristy said, "and he's a great guy."

"What about your father?" Joni asked. "How can you love your stepfather when you have a real father? Don't you love *him*?"

Kristy paused. For years she thought she hated her real father because of the way he walked out on the family. Then, not long ago, he came to Stoneybrook and saw her. She was surprised to discover that part of her still loved him, in spite of everything.

"My father will always be my father," she said slowly. "But Watson is my father too, because he's there every day caring about me." It isn't easy for Kristy to talk about this stuff, but Joni and Ewan needed some help.

Joni turned away from her stubbornly. "I hate Mrs. McGill."

"You wouldn't hate her if you knew her," Kristy said. "And besides, it's just one date. Your dad might date lots of women before he remarries."

"Yuck," Ewan said.

"He might never remarry," Kristy added.

This last statement brightened Joni's outlook a little. "That's true," she admitted hopefully. "He won't ever find another person as good as my mother, no matter how hard he tries."

"Maybe not," Kristy said. "Though, you know, he might find someone he likes in different ways."

"He won't," Joni said confidently.

Although she calmed down at that point, Joni wasn't as confident as she sounded. Kristy said that no matter how hard she tried to distract the kids with games, videos, and stories, Joni's eyes were glued to the clock. "What's taking him so long?" she wanted to know at only eight o'clock.

Ewan fell asleep at eight-thirty. Joni asked to stay up to read, as she had when I was there, and Kristy said yes. By the time Mr. Brooke returned home at twelve-thirty, Kristy was sure Joni was asleep. So she was shocked when Joni appeared on the stairs the moment her father came in. "It's about time!" she scolded him.

Mr. Brooke made light of it, but Kristy said he seemed annoyed with his daughter.

"Stacey," Kristy said to me later, "if your mother sees him again, you're going to have to have a serious talk with those kids. They are not going to make this easy. No way."

She was probably right. So I began trying to come up with the best possible words to make this okay for them. Mr. Brooke wasn't the kind of man I was about to let my mother lose just because his kids were making things hard.

Of course, I didn't know any of this until after I returned from New York. That Saturday I ice-skated in the afternoon with Ethan. Then I met Dad at his office. (Naturally, he was working on a Saturday.) We had an early dinner together and then Dad said he would drive me home. He had a business meeting in Boston early Monday morning, so he was headed in that direction anyway. He had booked a hotel room in Stoneybrook for that night. He'd drive the rest of the way to Boston on Sunday so he could visit friends there and be ready for his meeting bright and early on Monday.

As we drove up the Henry Hudson Parkway and left the city behind, I began to think about Mom's date and the possibility of her remarrying. I wouldn't be the first of my friends to go through it. Kristy's mom had remarried and so had Dawn's. I didn't think I'd mind having Mr.

Brooke as a stepfather. He was so nice. And it was cool that he was a writer.

"What's on your mind?" Dad asked.

I should have been honest with him, but I couldn't find the words. It might sound as if I were trying to replace him as my dad. That wasn't it at all, of course. But I didn't quite know how to talk about Mr. Brooke without hurting Dad's feelings. "Just daydreaming," I said instead.

"What's your mother been up to these days?" he asked.

"Uh . . . the usual."

When we pulled up to our house, Dad walked me to the front door. "I'll come in and say hi to your mom," he said. But when I unlocked the front door, the house was dark.

"Mom?" I called. No one answered.

"Where is she?" Dad said impatiently.

"She went to a play with a friend," I told him.

"A friend?" I nodded but didn't offer any more information. "Want me to stay with you until she comes back?" he offered.

"Dad, I'm thirteen. I baby-sit all the time," I assured him.

"Lock the door after I leave," he said. Then he gave me the phone number of the hotel where he'd be staying.

After he left, I realized I was pretty tired. It

was late, and ice-skating with Ethan all afternoon had been a lot of exercise. I went straight upstairs, changed, and flopped into bed. I turned off my lamp and lay in bed in the dark, my eyes wide open. Where *was* Mom? It wasn't incredibly late, but in the last year she'd been home by nine-thirty most nights.

Another five minutes passed and my eyes were still wide open. It was hopeless. I wouldn't sleep until Mom was home. There was no sense trying. I climbed out of bed, took my copy of *Pride and Prejudice* from my bedside table, and went downstairs to the living room.

I'd read only a page of it when I began to think about Elizabeth Bennett. She was ruining everything because she was so proud and had so many issues about Mr. Darcy. I wondered if Mom would be like Elizabeth and throw silly roadblocks in the path of this relationship. For some reason, I could imagine her doing that, though I hoped she wouldn't.

At twelve-twenty I heard Mom's key in the door. "Good night," she called to Mr. Brooke. "Stacey!" she exclaimed as she shut the door. "You're still up!"

"I couldn't sleep. You're kind of late, aren't you?" I said.

She laughed and came into the living room. "It's only twelve-twenty."

From the smile on her face I could see she'd

had a good time. Even so I asked, "How did it go?"

"It was really fun. The performance wasn't fabulous, but it wasn't embarrassing. Not nearly as terrible as John had led me to believe it would be. And everyone made a big fuss over him. I felt like a celebrity myself just because I was his date. We went to the cast party afterward, which was in a very elegant apartment. John signed his books for people and I met some fascinating actors and playwrights."

"That must have been great," I said.

"It was. It *really* was."

"Are you going to see him again?" I asked.

She nodded. "This Tuesday. We're just going to go to a movie. You'll get a sitting request from him at your meeting on Monday."

"I can do it if no one else wants to," I said as I headed up the stairs. "Are you coming up?"

"In a minute."

I got the feeling she wanted to be alone, maybe to think about the evening. I said good night and went to bed. As I fell asleep, I realized there was a smile on my face.

All that Sunday, Mom was in a great mood. She hummed as she cleaned the breakfast dishes and later she went out to have her nails done. While she was at her manicure, Kristy called and told me how upset Joni and Ewan were. "You know," I said, "Joni was acting strange last time I sat for them. Now I get it." I remembered how observant Joni was. She'd realized her father liked my mother at the same time I realized my mother liked her father. That's what her quiet moodiness had been about.

I considered telling Mom what Kristy had told me. But when she came home she was still smiling and humming and I couldn't bear to. Maybe Mr. Brooke would talk to his kids and straighten everything out.

By the time I arrived at school on Monday, I was looking forward to seeing my friends. Except for my phone conversation with Kristy, I hadn't been in touch with them all weekend. The first one I spotted was Mallory, far down the hall. Since her mother had met Mr. Brooke first, I wanted to talk to Mal to see if her mother had said anything about him.

Her arms were loaded with books. She spotted me waving to her and smiled.

Mal hadn't noticed Alan Gray, the most obnoxious boy in the eighth grade, walking toward her. But I did. And there was something about the way he was walking that I didn't like, as if he were up to no good.

And then I saw exactly what he was up to, and I didn't have time to stop it.

I yelled at Mal to look out just as Alan deliberately stepped into her path and knocked her bottom book sharply with his bent elbow, sending all her books hurtling into the air.

"Duck for cover!" Alan yelled at full volume. "Spaz Girl is on the warpath. Run for your lives!"

Kids in the hallway jumped back, laughing, as the books crashed to the floor around them. Poor Mallory was the only one who really had to duck since the books were dropping all around her.

I sprinted to her side. Her eyes were red as she held back tears. "Jerk!" I yelled at Alan. He sauntered away, smirking. "Are you okay?" I asked Mallory.

Mallory took off her glasses and briskly wiped her eyes with the palms of her hands. I scurried around, picking up the fallen books. Turning back to her I saw tears running down her cheeks.

"Alan is a moron," I grumbled.

"It's not just him," Mallory said, drying her eyes on her sleeve. "Every day somebody does something like this to me. I can't stand coming to school anymore."

"They'll forget about it soon," I said.

"That's what I thought last month, but they're not forgetting about it. The only thing that will help is if I get out of SMS altogether."

"Well, you can't quit school, so there's no sense —"

"I can," she cut me off.

"What? No you can't."

"I don't have to go to *this* school. There are other schools. I've talked to my parents. They're thinking about it."

"About changing your school?" I cried. This seemed so drastic. All Mallory's friends were here.

"Shannon goes to Stoneybrook Day School. She's happy there," Mallory said.

"That's a pretty expensive school," I reminded her.

"Maybe I could get a scholarship." I saw she'd given this some thought.

"From now on make sure you hang out with us, your friends," I suggested. "No one will bug you then."

"I can't be with you every second," she argued. (This was true.) "I'd better get to math," she said, taking her books from me.

"I'll walk with you," I offered, even though my class was in the opposite direction. I had to go with her because I had the awful feeling that if anyone else bugged Mallory just then, she'd walk out of SMS and never come back again.

As Mom predicted, Mr. Brooke called at our Monday afternoon meeting, looking for a sitter. Abby and I were free. Since I didn't want to hog all the Brooke jobs, I offered it to her. "You better take it," Abby said. "From what Kristy wrote in the notebook, I think you have to work things out with those kids."

So I arrived Tuesday night at the Brooke house, prepared for a long discussion. (Mom dropped me off and left from there with Mr. Brooke.)

"Hello," Joni greeted me stiffly as she walked past on her way to the kitchen. She took a bag of potato chips from the cupboard.

"Want to play Monopoly?" I suggested.

"I have homework," she said.

As she walked out of the kitchen, Ewan came in. "Hi, Stacey," he said. "Want to —"

"Ewan," Joni called frostily from the living room.

"Excuse me," he said, with extreme formality. He walked out of the kitchen with his shoulders squared and his back stiff. I smiled, but I wondered what was going on. It seemed that I was being iced out.

I went into the living room, but Ewan and Joni weren't there. I decided to look for them upstairs. Ewan wasn't in his room. Joni's door was shut.

"We're busy," she called when I knocked.

I opened the door anyway. Joni sat on the bed with Ewan by her side. His easy reader was on her lap. "When you see *t* and *h* together, it makes a *th* sound," she explained to him. They didn't even look up at me.

Suddenly, I was tongue-tied. What was I supposed to say to them, anyway? They now saw me as their enemy (or at least Joni did) and probably figured I stayed up nights with my mother plotting ways to steal their father from them and replace their mother.

I was stumped. What can you say when you're being iced out by two adorable kids?

Back downstairs, I took *Jacob Have I Loved* from my backpack. Before I opened it, though, I noticed that the door to Mr. Brooke's study was slightly ajar. I couldn't resist the temptation to take a peek inside.

It was exactly as I'd imagined an author's study to be. There were two desks against opposite walls. On one sat a computer. On the other was a gorgeous antique typewriter. Floor-to-ceiling bookshelves covered a third wall. They contained not only Mr. Brooke's novels but books by lots of different authors. The fourth wall was covered with framed paintings. They were abstract collages, all by the same artist. A framed poster advertising one of Mr. Brooke's mysteries hung over the computer. There was also a poster advertising the play Mom and he had just gone to see. I stepped into the room to study it. "A new work by acclaimed novelist J. B. Angel," the poster announced.

I have to say, I was impressed. Not many people I know have a study like this one. It seemed so sophisticated. It was clear that a creative, accomplished person worked there.

I wondered what had gone wrong with the Brookes' marriage. Mr. Brooke seemed so awesome that I couldn't imagine anyone wanting to leave him. He was friendly, caring, smart, handsome, successful — what more did his wife want? Maybe he was the one who wanted the divorce. That seemed more likely. Or maybe it was more complicated than that. As I knew from my own experience, divorce is rarely a simple thing.

For the rest of the evening, the kids avoided me. Ewan had a hard time — I could tell he wanted to talk. But every time he'd wander close to me, Joni swooped down on him and took him away with her. At last they went upstairs to get ready for bed. I checked on them fifteen minutes later. Ewan was sleeping and Joni was reading.

Mom and Mr. Brooke were both laughing and happy when they returned at about ten.

Mr. Brooke asked if I could sit again on Thursday. I could, but I asked him to call the

BSC to set it up. The members have all agreed not to book personal jobs on our own.

He called at 6:10 that next day, Wednesday. We were still hanging around Claudia's room after the meeting, talking. "Why can't that guy get the time right?" Kristy complained.

At school I'd told everyone how weird the job had been so now Mary Anne said, "Do you want to skip it, Stacey?"

"No. I think I better face this," I said.

"Your mother was asking my mother all about Mr. Brooke today," Mallory said. "It sounds kind of serious."

"Does your mother know anything about him?" I asked.

"Just that his wife left him because she thought being a mother and wife was standing in the way of her career."

I was surprised. *She'd* left *him.*

"Ew, that's cold," Abby commented.

"Mrs. Brooke told someone, who told my mother, that she, meaning Mrs. Brooke, said she was tired of standing in her husband's shadow," Mallory reported. "She said marriage and motherhood had ruined her modeling career, but she still had a chance to make it in show business."

"Those kids should be *glad* to have *your* mother around, Stacey," Abby said. "They'd probably get more care and attention from her than they get from their own mother."

"Yeah, but their mother is still their mother," I replied. "They're loyal to her. I understand that."

I took the job for that Thursday, determined to speak to the kids. The plan was for me to go to the Brookes' at around four, so that Mr. Brooke could work for awhile, then to stay while he picked up my mother and they went out to dinner.

Once again, I received a frosty hello from Ewan and Joni before they disappeared up the stairs. Mr. Brooke didn't seem to notice. He was about to go into his study when I stopped him.

"Could I speak to you, Mr. Brooke?" I asked.

"Sure. But please call me John. What's up?"

"The kids are upset that you're going out with my mother," I began. "And they're not crazy about me these days either, since I'm her daughter."

"Come on in," he said, gesturing toward his study. He offered me the chair in front of his computer. He sat backward on the chair by his typewriter. "The kids don't really understand what happened between me and my wife. They don't realize that I have custody of them because my wife doesn't want the responsibility. I didn't want them to know that.

Maybe, though, the time has come to explain some of it to them. Or at least to Joni, who's old enough to understand, I think."

"I don't want them to be upset," I said.

"Don't worry. I'll be tactful and gentle when I talk to Joni. Thanks for letting me know this." Mr. Brooke — John — stood up, which gave me the idea he wanted to get to work.

I left the study, glad that I'd spoken to him. I wouldn't try to talk to the kids until after their father had a chance to speak to them. Although it was unpleasant, I could stand one more night of the big chill.

As I sat on the couch with my book, I realized that John was easy to talk to. No wonder my mother liked him so much. I started imagining him as a stepfather. He'd probably be pretty cool. Mom and I would become famous, sort of, since he was famous.

A pang of guilt hit me. What about Dad? Was I being incredibly disloyal by even thinking about replacing him?

I pushed away the guilt. Dad was still my dad. And lots of kids had stepfathers and stepmothers. So, I thought, if I were possibly, someday, maybe going to have a stepfather, it might as well be one as interesting and nice as John.

"It was different for me," Mary Anne said at our meeting on Friday. "My mother was dead, and I'd never known her. So I didn't have the feeling that I was replacing someone I loved." We were talking about what it's like when one of your parents is dating. As you might guess, I brought up the topic. It seemed to be all I could think about.

"But it was still weird," Mary Anne continued. "I was never sure if Dad's girlfriends liked me or if they were only pretending to like me because of Dad."

"Did you feel that way about Sharon?" Jessi asked, referring to Dawn's mom, Mary Anne's stepmom.

"No. I felt she liked me right away. Up until he started seeing her, I didn't want him to remarry. Dad and I were doing all right by ourselves. I suppose I thought a stepmother would take my father away from me."

"What changed your mind?" Claudia asked.

"Dawn, of course. I was so excited about the idea of us becoming stepsisters that I forgot all my other worries." She stopped as a thoughtful expression came to her face. "It's funny the way it worked out," she continued after a moment. "I didn't especially want a stepmother, but I *did* want a stepsister. And now my stepsister is thousands of miles away for most of the year, but I have a wonderful stepmom. So — you never know how things are going to turn out."

"Tell me about it," Kristy said, leaning forward in Claudia's director's chair. "Remember how unsure I was about Watson?"

"I remember," Claudia said. "You didn't think your mother should marry him at all."

Kristy shook her head. "I know. Now I can't imagine why."

"You probably felt protective of your mother," I suggested.

"Could be. And I suppose it just takes awhile to really get to know someone."

"I wish my mother would date instead of being so involved with her job," Abby complained. "Even if Mr. Perfect showed up on her doorstep, she'd probably trample him on her way to the office."

"But do you really want a stepfather?" I asked.

"I don't know," Abby replied. "I don't think Mom would ever find anyone as cool as my father, but . . ." Her voice trailed off and I suspected she was remembering her dad.

At that moment, the phone rang, distracting us all from the conversation. It was Mrs. Rodowsky wanting a sitter for Shea, Archie, and Jackie for Sunday afternoon. While Mary Anne found a sitter, I thought about everything we'd been talking about.

Mary Anne and Abby had parents who had died. And Kristy's father was pretty much gone too. None of them had the expectation that their other parent might come back someday. I didn't either. I'd accepted that my parents were divorced for good.

I suddenly felt a lot of sympathy for Joni and Ewan. I realized they were younger, and the divorce had just happened. They didn't understand why their mother was gone. They didn't want her replaced before she had the chance to return.

"Mallory, how about you?" I heard Mary Anne say. "It's from noon to three. You could handle it."

"I can't," Mallory replied. "I'll be in Massachusetts."

"Massachusetts!" Kristy cried. "Why?"

All eyes turned to Mallory. She drew a deep breath before she spoke. "My parents and I want to see a boarding school there."

Everyone spoke at once, our voices tumbling over one another.

"Boarding school!"

"No way!"

"You can't!"

"Why?"

"I thought you wanted to go to Stoneybrook Day!" That was me. I wasn't as shocked as everyone else because of the conversation I'd had with Mal. Still . . . boarding school? It seemed pretty extreme.

The only one not crying out in dismay was Jessi. Her jaw had dropped and her eyes were wide with shock. She stared at her best friend, speechless.

While she tuned out all the noise, Mallory heard Jessi's silent outcry. She turned to her as if the rest of us weren't there. "You don't know how horrible it's been. I hate going to school. I have a stomachache every morning, and at night I cry, just thinking about what tomorrow will be like. Each day I hope it's going to be better, but something always happens. Someone knocks into me or calls me Spaz Girl. I can't stand it anymore."

Jessi was still speechless, so I spoke for her. "But why go to a boarding school, and so far away?" I asked.

"My parents can't afford Stoneybrook Day.

But I got on the Internet and researched schools offering scholarships. I found this school in Massachusetts that sounds *very* cool. I persuaded Mom to contact them by e-mail. She did and we've been communicating that way. It seems that I have a very good chance to win a scholarship because they were impressed with my writing awards."

Jessi finally found her voice, although it came out in a choked whisper. "It's so far away."

Mallory tried to smile but her expression was more an apologetic grimace than a grin. "Not *that* far. You can come visit. And I'll be home a lot, summers and holidays and all. Like Dawn."

I don't think that comparison cheered anyone. Dawn isn't completely gone — but it's not the same as having her here all the time.

"I might not even like it!" Mallory said, her voice rising defensively. "I could hate it. I'm only looking."

"You'll hate it," Jessi murmured, staring down at the rug. I felt terrible for her. She was losing her best friend. I can't imagine what I'd do if Claudia suddenly announced she was moving out of town, or even thinking about it.

A terrible silence fell over us. The idea of Mallory's leaving was awful. I wished I could come up with some other solution to her school problem. I couldn't, though, and I suppose no one else could think of one either. None of us wanted her to go on being miserable. Yet we didn't want her to leave.

"Someone better call back Mrs. Rodowsky," Kristy said at last, breaking the tension. "Who's taking the job?"

"Me, I guess," Mary Anne told her.

Claudia called Mrs. Rodowsky, since she'd taken the original call. When she was done, I sensed another big silence about to fall over us, so I jumped in. "What about our book group?" I reminded them. "Has everyone been reading *Jacob Have I Loved*?"

"I have," Mallory spoke up. "It's meant a lot to me because I understand how Louise feels. She's just got to get off that little island where they live and go somewhere else, but she's trapped in a place where she doesn't think anyone understands her or cares about her."

"How can you say that?" Jessi cried indignantly, rising to her knees. "We understand you. We care about you."

"And Louise is wrong," Abby added. "There are lots of people who care about her; she just doesn't see it."

"And in the end," Kristy added, "she doesn't —"

"Stop!" Mary Anne said sharply. "I'm nowhere near the end. Don't tell."

"Okay," Kristy said. She gazed pointedly at Mallory. "What I mean is, even though Louise *wants* to leave the island, it's not necessarily what she *should* do."

"Maybe," Mallory admitted. "But I'm not a character in a book. This isn't a story. I have to do what *I* think is best."

"Have you spoken to Joni and Ewan yet?" I asked Mr. Brooke — I mean, John — when I baby-sat at his house on Tuesday after school. The kids hadn't realized I was there yet. They were playing in the basement.

"Yes and no," he replied. "I talked, but I'm not sure they listened."

"Oh," I said glumly. I'd arrived there hoping that the kids would feel better about everything. "Well, maybe some of it sunk in," I suggested, trying to sound encouraging.

He nodded but didn't appear convinced. "They do understand that no amount of bad attitude on their part is going to stop me from seeing your mom," he added firmly. "Maureen is a terrific woman. So smart and funny."

"She's pretty amazing," I agreed.

"She's beyond amazing," he said, heading toward his study. He planned to work for two hours, then pick up Mom to go to dinner. "She's . . . she's *luminous.*"

"Luminous?"

"Yes, she shines with an inner light."

"She does?"

He laughed. "She does. She has an inner glow. Look more closely next time you see her."

He disappeared into his study, and I made a mental note to check Mom for signs of glowing. As far as I was concerned this was going extremely well. John was wild about Mom, and that was fine with me.

That night, Ewan sat close beside me while we watched TV together. I think he simply couldn't keep up with Joni's campaign against me. He was too young to stay angry when he didn't fully understand what he was supposed to be angry about.

While he sat there, Joni glared at him from her spot on the floor. He wasn't aware of her, but I was. And when I got up to go to the bathroom, I heard her hiss the word *traitor* at him sharply. When I came back, he was glued to his sister's side, on the floor, and wouldn't look at me.

The evening went on pretty much in that way. Things were the same when I sat for them on Thursday. (The BSC members had decided to give me all the Brooke jobs, so I'd have a chance to work this out.)

Once again, John and Mom were going out, this time to the movies. And, once again, I was getting mixed messages from Ewan and the deep freeze from Joni, the human ice storm. "Come on, Joni, give me a break," I pleaded at one point.

Her face softened, and, for a moment, I thought she was going to say something without a snap in her voice. Then her large green eyes shifted to the picture of the kids with their mother that stood on the TV. Her face hardened again. Without a word to me, she walked upstairs.

I sighed. At least Ewan relaxed and smiled at me once Joni was gone. We turned off the TV and worked on a house of cards together. From time to time, Joni came halfway down the stairs, glared at us, and left. When I checked on her, I found her in the living room, sitting on the couch, intently writing a letter on unicorn-bordered stationery. She never even looked up, pretending not to know I was there.

That night, as I rode home from the Brookes' house with Mom, I tried to get some idea of how she felt about Mr. Brooke. "John's great, isn't he?" I said.

"Very nice," she replied. I'd expected more. After all, he thought she was beyond amazing — luminous.

"Nice?"

Mom nodded. "And intelligent."

Of course he's intelligent. He's an author and a playwright. Anyone would know he's intelligent. "Would you say he's a genius?" I probed.

She turned to me with a surprised smile. "Why would you think he's a genius?"

"Not everyone can write books," I reminded her.

"No . . . but that doesn't make him a genius."

"Don't you think he's smart?"

"Yes. I said he was intelligent."

"More intelligent than Dad?"

My own words shocked me. I couldn't believe they'd actually come from my mouth. What did it matter if he was more or less intelligent than my father?

"I can't say," Mom answered as we pulled into the driveway. "Your father is analytical and highly logical. John is so creative. They have very different kinds of intelligence."

I liked that answer. It made them equal but different. Impossible to compare. "Was his play brilliant?" I asked.

"Not especially," she said, getting out of the car.

"But you told him it was good. I heard you."

"Good, but not brilliant. There were some stretches of dialogue I thought were trite. And there were some philosophical positions I didn't agree with."

We walked together into the kitchen by the side door. I had no idea what she was talking about — philosophical positions? "Do you mean you didn't agree with what he had to say?" I asked.

"Yes."

"Those were only his characters talking," I said.

"A dramatist speaks through his characters."

"Not all of them," I pointed out.

"Well, his main character voiced some world views I don't agree with. The main character acted and looked and seemed a lot like John."

"What kind of world views?" I demanded to know.

She thought a moment. "Well, that . . . that people are basically selfish and are always motivated by what's best for them. I think that's untrue and somewhat distasteful."

"You seemed so happy when you came home from the play," I reminded her.

"I was happy," she said as she took off her jacket and hung it in the closet. "I had a great time. It's just that I've had some time to think about the play since then. And I'm reading John's other books and seeing that theme again and again. I'm sorry, but it disturbs me."

"Oh, that's nothing to worry about," I assured her. "That's writing. Your relationship with him is real life."

"The literature that he creates comes from what's in his head."

"Who cares if he thinks people are generally rotten?" I said. "He thinks you're wonderful. He told me you're luminous."

"He said that?" she asked as a smile spread across her face. And guess what. I saw it on her face. She *was* glowing from within. He was right.

Mom and I had a cup of herbal tea together at the kitchen table. I warned her about Joni. I felt she ought to know.

"John told me about that tonight," Mom said. "We came up with a plan. Tomorrow night we're going to dinner, all of us. You can come, can't you?"

"Sure. I can come." In fact, nothing could have stopped me. This was great. Even if Mom thought John was less than brilliant and had a rotten "world view," she was getting serious. I'd seen how she glowed at his compliment. Plus, she wouldn't want to go out with his kids if the relationship weren't going somewhere. I was *sure* we were on the right track.

On Friday, we went to Pietro's, an Italian restaurant on the way to Washington Mall.

John and the kids pulled into the parking lot at the same time Mom and I arrived. "Are you ready for this?" she asked me with a wry smile.

"I am. Are you?" Although Mom had been introduced to the kids, I knew them better than she did. I knew what to expect.

"Probably not," she said, reapplying her lipstick in the rearview mirror. "But we're here now. Let's do it." She and I got out of the car and joined the Brooke family.

"Hi, ladies," John greeted us warmly.

"Hello, John," Mom said with her eyes on the kids. "Joni, Ewan, how are you tonight?"

"Fine," Joni snapped, not making eye contact with Mom or me.

"I'm hungry," Ewan announced with more warmth.

The restaurant was crowded and noisy. We were seated at a large round table in the middle of the dining room. "Those are great earrings, Maureen," John said as the waiter passed us the menus.

With her hand, Mom touched one of the Venetian glass beaded earrings she wore. "Oh, thanks. I like them too."

"I know why you like them, Dad," Joni spoke up. "They're almost exactly like the ones you gave Mom for Christmas last year. Only my mother's beads are nicer colors. Mrs.

McGill, did your ex-husband give you those beads?"

Wow! I thought, staring at Joni. *This kid is going right for the kill.* She was good at it too.

I had a feeling Dad *had* given Mom the earrings for her birthday one year. (I recalled that he mailed them to her because he was out of town on business. Typical.) "I've had these a long time," Mom said, dodging the question.

"And besides, it's none of your business," John said pointedly to Joni. "What are you going to order?"

"I don't know. The food here stinks."

"You've never eaten here," John reminded her.

With a shrug, she covered her face with the menu. "Everyone says it does," she replied from behind it.

John rolled his eyes at Mom and she smiled at him. In a few minutes, the waitress came for our order. When she left, we had nothing to do but talk. Only no one said anything. "How's your book coming, John?" I asked in an effort to fill the silence.

"I don't know," he answered. "I can never tell until I'm finished."

"My mother always read what he wrote and told him how to fix it," Joni volunteered. "She practically wrote his books herself."

"Joni!" John said, looking hurt. "That's not true."

"She said it was."

"I'm sure every writer can use another eye on his or her work," Mom spoke up, trying to smooth things.

"That's true. I wonder if you'd have the time to look at the manuscript I'm working on now," John said.

Mom looked trapped. "I'd be glad to read it, but —"

"She doesn't know how!" Joni cried indignantly. "That's Mom's job."

"Joni!" John said sharply.

"That's all right," Mom said. "She's right. I'm not an editor and —"

"And you're not his wife!" Joni cut her off.

John abruptly pushed back his chair and eyed his daughter angrily. "Joni, I've had just about enough of this."

Tears sprang to her eyes. She stood, knocking her chair backward into the table behind us as she ran from the dining room.

Mom looked at John, expecting him to follow her. My eyes were on Ewan, who was misty-eyed and wore a panicked expression. John sat firmly in his chair, red-faced with anger.

"I'd go get her, but I don't think she'd want to talk to me," Mom said. I knew it was her way of suggesting John go.

"Let her be," John said, pulling in his chair. "If she wants to miss dinner, that's her choice.

But she's not going to spoil it for the rest of us."

I knew Mom wasn't happy with that decision. "I'll go," I offered. "Maybe I can talk to her." Hurrying through the restaurant, I found Joni sitting on a chair in the lobby, fuming. "Come on, Joni," I said. "Come back to the table."

"Why should I?" she snapped, folding her arms.

"Mom and I just want to be friends with you guys. It's no big deal. You don't have to get all defensive about it," I said.

"Liar. You don't want to be friends. You want your mother to marry my father."

Maybe I did, and maybe I didn't. It was too early to say for sure. But there was no sense telling her that just then. "It's too soon for them to be thinking about marriage," I said.

Before Joni could reply, John appeared in the lobby. "Joni, get back to the table this instant," he said.

"No."

He came close to her and took hold of her arm. "You get back there now, and you show Maureen some respect, or you will be grounded without TV for the rest of the week. Got that?"

If I were her, I would have gotten it. He was so quietly enraged that it was a little scary.

She got the message. Drawing her mouth

into a tight, angry line and holding her head high, she rose from the chair and walked stiffly back into the dining room. Her exaggerated dignity would have been cute if the situation hadn't been so exasperating.

To my surprise, John turned to me and smiled his megawattage smile. How could he shift gears so quickly? "Kids," he said to me, as if this weren't really such a big deal, after all. "What are you going to do with them?"

I shrugged and felt relieved by the light spin he'd just put on things.

By the time we returned to the table, the food had arrived. Thank goodness! Each of us threw ourselves into eating, as if we were starved. Joni didn't say one more thing for the rest of the evening.

Ewan talked a little about school, but I wasn't one bit surprised when everyone turned down dessert.

In the parking lot, Mom and John held hands as we walked to our cars. As awful as the evening had been, it had brought them closer.

"I've been thinking," John said as we were about to separate. "Thanksgiving is coming up. Maureen, you said you didn't have plans. Neither do we. Why don't we spend Thanksgiving together?"

Joni went pale, and I seriously worried that she might faint.

"I don't know." Mom hesitated, looking at the Brooke kids.

John broke out into the big smile again and put his arm around Mom. "Sure you do," he insisted. "It'll be fun."

"It'll be great," I seconded. I realized John and I were on the same team. We were both pushing for this relationship and we weren't going to let anything stop us.

"I suppose," Mom gave in. "All right."

I smiled . . . while Joni looked at Mom with murder in her eyes.

Monday

You have to say this about Joni Brooke— she's one determined kid. She should join the marines when she's older because she sure knows how to put up a fight. Good Luck, Stacey. You'll need it. I wouldn't want her mad at me for anything.

Abby told me that her first reaction to Joni was horror mixed with deep admiration. (I'd asked Abby to take the job because I needed a break from Joni.) "She must be a descendant of Genghis Khan," she joked with me at our meeting that afternoon. "Maybe she *was* Genghis Khan in another lifetime."

"Why," I asked, laughing. "What happened?"

Abby told me she arrived at the Brooke house after school and immediately sensed that John was very tense. She'd never met him before, but his pinched expression didn't match the impression I'd given her of him. "I should warn you," he explained, "I've just had a talk with Joni about some things she and I need to straighten out. I'm not sure it went too well."

"Was it about Mrs. McGill?" Abby asked. I'd never have been so blunt, but Abby speaks right out when she has a question.

John didn't seem to mind. "Yes, in fact, it was," he said as he headed for his study to work. "She has to realize that her mother and I are divorced and I like Maureen very much. All her foolish tirades aren't going to change that."

"But she didn't want to hear it?" Abby ventured.

"No, I'm afraid not. She and Ewan are down

in the basement now. If I let you leave at five-fifteen, will that give you enough time to get to your meeting?"

"Sure," Abby said. "That will be fine." When John had gone into his study, Abby went downstairs. The TV was on, but the kids weren't watching it. Ewan was putting together a puzzle on the floor.

Joni sat cross-legged on the couch, mashing a lump of yellow Play-Doh in her hands. She looked up as Abby came down the stairs. "Thank goodness," she said sourly. "At least you're not Stacey."

"No, last time I looked, I was Abby. Hi, guys."

Ewan smiled up at her. "Want to help me with this puzzle?"

Abby sat down and began piecing it together with him. "Are you Stacey's friend?" Joni asked.

"Yes," Abby replied. "She's really a terrific person." Joni snorted contemptuously. "You should give her a chance," Abby continued. "Mrs. McGill too. You'd like them."

"It's her fault we never see our father, ever," Joni accused. "He can't work at night when we're asleep because he has to take *her* out. So he has to work now, while we're awake. Thanks to her, we don't have a mother *or* a father."

"Whoa," said Abby. "None of that is Mrs. McGill's fault."

Joni didn't seem to hear her. She was suddenly bright-eyed but far away, as if she were working out some new exciting idea.

"What?" Abby asked. "What are you thinking?"

Joni hopped off the couch. "If Dad couldn't work in the afternoons, then he would have to get his work done at night," she said, talking to herself more than to Abby. "And if he has to work at night, then he can't take out . . ." She let her voice trail off. "I have to go do something," she said.

Abby didn't like the sound of that. She stood up. "What do you have to do?"

"Something," Joni replied, already halfway up the stairs.

"Be right back," Abby told Ewan. She ran upstairs behind Joni. She was at the top of the stairs when she heard the radio in the living room blaring hard rock. John came flying out of his study, just as Abby came racing into the living room.

"Joni!" he bellowed, snapping off the radio. He and Abby both looked around but didn't see her.

Abby felt embarrassed that she'd lost track of her charge. "She can't have gone far," she said. As she spoke, the door to John's study slammed shut.

John sprinted to his study, but when he tried to open the door, he found that it was locked. He banged on it. "Open up, young lady!" He tried being firm. Then he tried being nice. Nothing worked. "This is ridiculous," he fumed, storming out the front door.

Abby stood there, feeling helpless. She had no idea what would happen next. Ewan came up to see what the yelling was about. Abby was about to explain when she heard the sound of a window opening from within the study. The next thing she knew, Joni came flying out of the study and raced out the front door.

John lunged out of his office, looking wild. "She unplugged the mouse from my computer and took it!" he cried. "Where did she go with it?" His eyes darted around the room. "Where is she? I need that computer today. I'm done with the typewriter. I can't believe this kid!"

Abby headed for the front door. "She went outside. I'll find her." She ran out with Ewan beside her. "There she is," she cried, spying Joni down the block, standing on the corner. Abby sprinted to her. "You better give your father back that mouse," she said. "He's good and mad."

"I can't," Joni said.

"Of course you can," Abby blurted out. Glancing over her shoulder, she saw John barreling down the street toward them. Joni just shook her head and craned her neck back to look up at the tall, bare maple beside them. Abby followed her gaze and gasped. The mouse dangled on its cord from a high branch.

"Good throw," Ewan said.

Joni saw her father and took off around the corner. John reached Abby and Ewan a second later. "Did she give you the mouse?" he demanded.

Cringing, Abby pointed up to the branch. John saw it and his face turned redder than she'd ever seen anyone's face become. Then he began breathing deeply and slowly, forcing himself to calm down. "She doesn't want you to work during the day," Abby explained, "because then you'll have to work at night and you won't be able to take out Mrs. McGill."

To her surprise and relief, John began to chuckle, though his face was still pretty red. "Okay," he said. "I'm going to go to the computer store and buy another mouse. You and Ewan see if you can catch up with her and bring her home. Tell her, by the way, that she's in deep trouble."

"Okay," Abby agreed. John walked back toward the house and Abby set off, with Ewan, down the block. She spotted Joni cowering in the bushes of a neighbor's house. "Come on out," Abby told her.

Joni's head slowly emerged and she checked around carefully for her father. When she didn't see him, she crawled all the way out. "Your plan worked for now," Abby informed her. "But your dad isn't taking Mrs. McGill out tonight anyway."

Joni smiled knowingly. "Yes, but they're going out tomorrow. If I keep this up, he'll be so behind schedule he'll have to cancel their date. The other day I wrote a letter to my mother telling her what's going on. I bet she'll come back when she reads it. Once she's back, all this will go away."

"Why didn't you just tell her on the phone?" Abby asked.

Joni was walking ahead of Abby and Ewan. "Oh, she doesn't call," she said. "She's busy in the evening working on her new show. So I write to her. She sends postcards and little notes back."

Abby gazed down at Ewan and ruffled his hair. "This is a hard time for you guys, isn't it?" she said sympathetically.

Ewan shrugged. "I guess."

Abby and Ewan began to walk home together, with Joni about a half block ahead. Suddenly Joni broke into a run and raced into the house, shutting the door behind her. Quickening her pace, Abby hurried Ewan along.

When they reached the front door it was

locked. Abby banged on it. "Joni!" She leaned on the bell. "Open up!" She raced around to the back door, and discovered that it was locked too. She tried the study window, but Joni had thought to fasten it. After leaning on the bell a bit longer, Abby gave up. She and Ewan settled down on the steps to await John's return. "Your father must have a set of house keys, right?" she said to Ewan.

"I don't know," Ewan answered.

Luckily, John *did* have his house keys. But, when they got inside, they discovered that Joni had deleted the entire chapter John had just finished. He was incredibly upset for a moment. Then he recalled a way he could find the file in his computer, and was able to get it back.

Still, he was not a happy camper. When he found Joni sitting in her closet reading a book, he grounded her for a million years or "until I say differently!"

I listened to Abby's story and sighed. Joni's cold war was beginning to heat up.

Chapter 10

Mom took a vacation day on the Wednesday before Thanksgiving to prepare for our double-family feast. "I have lots of vacation time, so I might as well use it," she said. Her voice was cheerful . . . too cheerful. Nervously cheerful.

I suppose it made sense. She was preparing a first-time holiday meal for a man she was dating. And his kids.

"Don't let Joni and Ewan get to you, Mom," I said as we sat together in the kitchen that afternoon, peeling sweet potatoes. "They'll behave."

Mom smiled ruefully. "You know why John and I didn't go out last night, don't you?"

After what Abby had told me, I had a hunch. "He had to work?"

She nodded. "He had to work because the day before, Joni stole his mouse, then locked him out of the house and attempted to delete the chapter he was writing. By the time he found it, Abby had to leave. Then the next afternoon, Joni inserted a password into the program containing John's book and hid from him for the rest of the day. By the time he found her and got her to reveal the password, it was time for our date and he had to cancel."

"Smart kid," I commented.

"Too smart," Mom said, shaking her head. "I sympathize with her, though. Imagine what she must be going through."

"I went through it," I reminded her.

"I know, sweetie, but you were a little older. And I think you knew both your parents were still your parents. Her mother has more or less left them on their own. John says she drops them the occasional postcard, but that's about it."

There was a knock on the kitchen door. I opened it and let Mallory in. (The Pikes live in the house behind ours.) "Hi," she said. "Mom wants to know if you have an electric beater. Ours conked out while she was preparing her cake mix."

Mom put down a sweet potato and stood up to check the cabinet over the stove. "I haven't used it in ages. But I think it's here," she said as she rummaged through the pans.

I hadn't talked much with Mallory since her weekend in Massachusetts. "What did you think of the school?" I asked. She hadn't really talked about it at Monday's BSC meeting.

"It's in the Berkshires, this beautiful hilly part of Massachusetts," she told me. "And the school is really pretty too. It's close to some cool-looking riding stables. I've always wanted to take riding lessons again."

Her last statement worried me. "Then . . . you're going?"

"Not definitely, but maybe. It's possible."

"But you belong here," I said.

"I don't belong at SMS. If I did, I wouldn't be so miserable there. But nothing is definite yet. It's something to think about, though."

"Boarding school," I said. "The idea of it is so odd."

"There are lots of girls there my age," Mallory pointed out. "They all looked happy to me. And the school isn't your typical boarding school. It focuses on the creative arts and community service. It's pretty cool."

Mom handed Mallory the electric beater. "Have a nice Thanksgiving," she said to her. "Tell your parents and brothers and sisters to come by tomorrow if they'd like. Claire is in Ewan's class, and Vanessa is Joni's age. They might know one another from school."

Mallory stared at me in pretend horror. "The *Brooke* kids will be *here*? Good luck."

"Thanks," I said with a laugh. "We'll be fine."

"Sure you will," Mallory said doubtfully.

When she opened the door to leave, John was there, his arm raised, about to ring the bell.

"Hi," he said, stepping into the kitchen. Mom ran her hand through her hair and smiled a little nervously at him. He'd taken her completely by surprise.

Mallory stood behind him and mouthed the word *cute* before leaving.

"I'm on my way out to the stores," John explained, "and I wanted to know what you need me to bring tomorrow."

"Uh . . . nothing," Mom said. "Just yourselves."

"No, come on, that's not fair. What do you need?" John insisted. I noticed he held a large manila envelope in his hand. I wondered what was in it.

"Bring things Joni and Ewan like," Mom suggested. "How are they feeling about tomorrow?"

"Oh, you know, whatever. . . . We'll have a good time."

"It's that bad, eh?" Mom said.

"Oh, I can't worry about it anymore. Life goes on. Joni will just have to get that through her head." He thought a moment. "How about this? I'll cover dessert and appetizers."

"Okay," Mom agreed.

"What's in the envelope?" I asked, unable to contain my curiosity any longer.

"Oh, gee, I almost forgot." John offered the envelope to Mom. "This is my book so far. I was wondering if you could look it over for me, give me your opinion."

Mom took the envelope from him, but she didn't take it eagerly. "Well . . . sure . . . but how soon do you need it back?"

"No hurry," he told her. "A week, a week and a half?" Mom nodded and John aimed that gorgeous smile of his at her. "Thank you. Really." He clapped his hands briskly. "Let me go before the stores are completely mobbed."

Mom watched him leave and stared at the door after he'd closed it behind him. "Do you believe that?" she asked.

"Believe what?"

"Here I am in the middle of Thanksgiving preparations and he hands me one more chore to do." She dropped the envelope onto the kitchen table.

"He didn't ask you to do it this instant," I pointed out. "This is a *good* thing. It shows he trusts your opinion."

"This is something his wife used to do," Mom said.

"So? That's good too, isn't it?"

My mother looked at me questioningly. "Do you think he wears tinted contacts?"

"I don't know," I replied, surprised. "Joni has the same green eyes."

"Yes, but his are greener."

"Is that bad?"

She shook her head. "I suppose not. It seems a little vain in a man. It makes me wonder if he dyes his hair. It's awfully free of gray, don't you think?"

It hadn't crossed my mind. I guess a guy his age should have had more gray. "Does any of that matter, Mom?" I asked her. "So what if he wants to look good? We all like to, don't we?"

"Yes, maybe I'm being old-fashioned."

"You are," I assured her. She had a real case of the jitters. I kept my fingers crossed that everything would go smoothly the next day.

On Thanksgiving morning, Mom dropped her best serving bowl on the kitchen floor. It shattered into a billion pieces. "I'll clean it up," I told her as I rushed into the kitchen to see what had crashed. "I'm sorry. I know you liked that bowl."

"This is not a good sign," Mom said, reaching in the closet for the broom.

I took it from her. "Don't be superstitious. Every year something breaks. You said so yourself."

After we'd swept up, Mom and I set the table together. Mom was very quiet. As we worked, though, she seemed to calm down. "You're right," she said at one point, although I hadn't said a word in nearly fifteen minutes. "This is Thanksgiving and we're having friends over. No big deal."

"Right," I agreed with a smile. "No biggie."

We expected the Brookes at noon. At a quarter to twelve the bell rang. "He's always either early or late," Mom muttered as she yanked off her apron and checked herself in the front hall mirror before opening the door. "Hello, come in," she said warmly.

Joni and Ewan wandered into our front hall as if they had just landed on an alien planet and were surveying the strange terrain. They were very cautious but extremely interested. Their eyes drank in each picture, every piece of furniture.

John was laden with brown paper bags. Mom took some from him. "What is all this?" she laughed. "I cooked, you know. You didn't have to bring your own meal."

"The Native Americans didn't come to the feast empty-handed," he said, smiling.

"Does that make Mom and me Pilgrims?" I asked.

"I suppose it does. The best-looking Pilgrims I've ever seen."

"Oh, puh-lease." Joni groaned. Everyone ignored her.

Mom took their coats and hung them in the closet. "Stacey, maybe Joni and Ewan would like to see the rest of the house," she suggested.

"Sure," I said. "Come on, guys, I'll show you around." I was surprised when Ewan took my hand. Happily surprised. I led the kids upstairs. Joni hung back but followed. "This is where I sleep," I said when we came to my room.

"This is nice," Joni said, walking right in and looking around.

"Thanks." I suddenly remembered the sharp, interested Joni I'd met the first day I sat for the kids. The high-spirited girl who noticed everything. She stopped at my desk and gazed down at a necklace I'd bought from a street vendor the last time I was in New York City. It was a carved wooden elephant strung on a satin cord. "Would you like to try it on?" I offered.

Her eyes lit up. "Could I?" I helped her put it on and steered her toward my dresser mirror. She fingered the wooden elephant. "It's cool."

"Keep it," I said. Okay, maybe I was too eager to win her over. But this seemed to be working, and the vendor stood on the same corner every day. I could replace the necklace.

"Are you sure?" she asked. "I shouldn't take your necklace."

"No, really. It looks great on you," I insisted. I looked at Ewan and wondered what I could give him. "Hey, Ewan, I have something for you too." I took my Kid-Kit from the closet and found a brand-new coloring book and pack of crayons. "Here, take these," I offered.

"Thank you," he said happily.

The kids were actually smiling at me. What a

relief. "I'll show you the rest of the house," I said.

After the tour we joined Mom and John in the living room. I noticed that Mom had set out a big dish of cold cooked shrimp, which John had brought, along with lots of cheese, fruit, and crackers.

"Help yourselves to appetizers," Mom offered. "Would you kids like some soda or juice?"

Ewan asked for juice.

"I'll just have the food my father brought," Joni said, loading a plate with cheese and crackers. She sat next to John on the couch and ate.

"Nice necklace," John commented.

"Stacey gave it to me," she said, not looking at him. Mom and John exchanged a meaningful glance. John shot me a thumbs-up when Joni wasn't looking.

After that, I went outside with the kids to play catch. Mallory and her brothers and sisters came by, which was great, because we were able to have a big game of touch football in the yard. Before we knew it, Mom was calling us in to eat. Joni and Ewan were panting and smiling (and slightly dirty) when they went inside.

We washed our hands and sat down. The mouthwatering aroma of turkey wafted into the dining room from the kitchen. Mom had filled her best vase with gorgeous maroon and yellow chrysanthemums and placed it in the middle of the table. The golden afternoon sunlight streamed through the window and made her good dinnerware and glasses gleam. Bowls of vegetables sat on the table, smelling delicious. She'd put a CD in the stereo, a lively piece of classical music, Vivaldi's *The Four Seasons.* To me, it was a perfect Thanksgiving setting.

"Do we have to listen to this?" Joni asked.

"Yes," John said.

"No," Mom replied at the same time. "What would you like to hear?"

"Hanson?" she suggested.

Mom looked at me. "I don't have anything by them," I said. "But I have plenty of other CDs."

"Wait a minute!" John broke in. "We're listening to this. I happen to like it very much."

"You're just saying that because *she* put it on," Joni argued. "You hate this kind of music."

"No, I don't."

"John, it's really no problem to change it," Mom said. "Stacey and I have lots of recordings. Stacey, go get some CDs to —"

"No," John cut her off firmly. "This music is fine." He rose from his chair. "Let me go get that turkey for you."

He and Mom hurried into the kitchen. I heard them exchange quick, anxious words, but I couldn't make out what they were saying. Joni sat at the table looking sullen. "I'd like to hear the Teletubbies," Ewan offered. "You don't have anything by them, do you?"

"I don't think so," I said. "Maybe we could borrow something from the Pikes after dinner."

Mom and John returned with the carved turkey. "Do you like the light meat or the dark, Joni?" Mom asked.

"I'm not eating that," she said.

"And why not?" John demanded.

"I'm a vegetarian."

"Since when? I noticed you scarfing down all the bacon this morning at breakfast."

She glared at him through angry slitted eyes. "That turkey is disgusting. I'm not eating it."

"That's it, Joni!" John barked. His voice rose to a fierce shout that made goose bumps form on my arms. "You're ruining Thanksgiving for everyone and I won't allow it."

Joni jumped to her feet. Tears sprang to her eyes and she bolted from the room.

I stood outside my bedroom door and knocked. I'd followed Joni up the stairs and reached the top in time to see her disappear into my room, slamming the door behind her.

"Go away!" Joni sobbed from the other side.

"It's me. Stacey." I hoped that would make a difference. Slowly the door opened. Joni's face was puffy and red from crying.

I stepped into my room and shut the door again. "I'll give you back your necklace," Joni said, pulling it over her head.

"I don't want it back," I told her. "I gave it to you because I like you. I think you're a good kid."

"You do not."

I sat on my bed. "I met you before our parents got together, remember? I know how you really are. Joni, my parents are divorced too. I understand what you're going through."

She buried her face in her hands and began

crying even harder. Her face was crushed into an expression of so much pain I practically felt it myself. It brought back terrible memories of feelings and fears from my own past. I remembered the horrible loneliness of lying in the dark, wondering how such an awful thing could be happening to me. I felt as if the whole world were cracking apart. And I wondered how I would survive.

I wasn't sure if Joni would let me hug her, but I took a chance and wrapped my arms around her. She collapsed into me, soaking my shoulder with tears. I squeezed her tight. She felt like a small, trembling bird.

"It gets better, Joni. I swear, it does." This was the only promise I could make. "The pain lessens and you make a new life."

"Why . . . did she . . . go?" Joni choked her words out through choppy breath. "How . . . could . . . she?"

I didn't know. "You should ask her someday," I suggested softly. I hoped that once their mother was settled, the kids would see and hear more from her. But that was a promise I couldn't make.

I went to the dresser for a box of tissues. "Listen, Joni, no matter how your father feels about your mother, it won't change how he feels about you and Ewan," I said, handing her the tissues. "You'll always be his kids and he loves you so much."

"He hates me," she sniffed, wiping her nose.

Despite the sadness of the moment, I laughed grimly. "He doesn't hate you," I said. "You've just been driving him crazy and he's fed up with the things you've been doing."

Joni smiled ruefully. "I *have* been pretty terrible."

"He gets mad, but I'm sure he understands," I said.

A knock came at the door and Mom stuck her head in. "Can I help?" she asked.

I didn't think she could. "We'll be down in a minute," I assured her. She nodded and left. "What do you say?" I asked. "Want to try again? You don't have to eat the turkey. There's lots of other stuff to eat."

"I like turkey," she admitted. That made us both smile.

"Come on," I said. "Let's go back."

She nodded and we returned to the dining room. We were met with the odd sight of Mom, John, and Ewan all eating in silence. The music had been turned off. Mom looked up and smiled softly at us. John kept eating.

"Hey, Joni, the turkey is good," Ewan said enthusiastically. "You should have some even if you are a vegetable now."

That caused smiles all around.

"A *vegetarian,*" she corrected him. "Not a vegetable. Okay, I'll have some."

The rest of the meal was somewhere between okay and not too bad — but not great. It surprised me that Mom and John were the two who seemed the most tense with each other. I don't think they exchanged a word for the rest of the meal. I wondered what had happened while I was upstairs with Joni.

The Brookes stayed for dessert. Joni even offered to help with the dishes. When we were finished, we left the kitchen and found John on the couch with Ewan asleep beside him. He picked up Ewan and let him sleep on his shoulder. "Thanks for everything," he said. "I think we'd better get going."

Mom got their coats and we walked the Brookes to the door. " 'Bye, Stacey. 'Bye, Mrs. McGill. Thank you," Joni said at the door.

"You're very welcome," Mom told her. She gave Joni a light hug and Joni didn't seem to mind.

John caught my eye and smiled. I smiled back at him. He'd scared me a little at the dinner table. But once again, he and I were on the same team, happy that things were finally working out.

"Thank goodness that's over," Mom said after we shut the door and the Brookes were in their car.

"It was pretty tense," I admitted. "But a lot of good things came out of it. You saw how much better Joni was after she came downstairs, didn't you?"

Mom stroked my hair. "You're a wonder, Stacey. What did you say to her?"

"Just that I understood a lot of her feelings."

Mom nodded. "They're really sweet kids. Their mother must have done something right."

"What about John?" I reminded her. "He's a great father."

"Do you think so?"

"Of course! Don't *you* think so?"

She sighed and shook her head. Then without saying anything, she began walking up the stairs.

"Mom!" I cried, trailing after her into her bedroom. "How can you think that? He's great with those kids."

"He's too tough on Joni. She's a little girl who has just gone through a terrible trauma. He's so impatient."

"Yeah, but he gets over it. Abby said that when Joni threw his mouse into the tree, he actually chuckled."

"Yes, and later he grounded her."

"She was terrible that day. He would have been a bad father if he had let her get away with everything," I countered.

Mom sat on her bed looking pale and tired.

"You'll see, the next time will be better," I said. "Now that Joni has a better attitude, our next dinner will be much better."

"I don't think there will be any more dinners," Mom said evenly. "I'm going to tell John this isn't working."

My jaw dropped. Was she crazy? "Why?" I blurted out.

"There are things that bother me about him. Did you notice that he didn't bother to offer to help with the dishes? Who does he think he is — the king? What kind of obnoxious macho example is that for Ewan?"

"That's a little thing," I argued. "You could mention it to him and he might change. But —"

"There are other things," she cut me off. "I think he's a charming but self-centered person. I don't want to be with someone like that. Not again. Your father was involved with his work and John is involved with John."

"Mom, you're just making excuses," I said angrily. "He's a great guy! He's your Mr. Darcy!"

"No, he's not."

"How do you know?"

"Stacey," she snapped. "I don't tell you who to date! Don't tell me!"

"You won't even give him a chance!" I yelled as I stormed out of her room. I couldn't believe my own mother could be so stupid.

It was a good thing I'd planned to go into Manhattan the next day to see Dad for the weekend. Mom had taken Friday off from work, and if she and I had been around each other too much that day we would have had a giant fight for sure.

I was so angry with her. The way I saw it, everyone else was trying like crazy to make her relationship with John work. Even Joni had started to try. Everyone was giving it a chance — except her. All she could do was study John and search for faults in him.

So what if he wore tinted contact lenses? Was that a crime? And she wasn't even sure he did! And I bet if she'd said, "John, could you help with the dishes?" he would have. He could have had his reasons for not helping. Maybe he wanted to give Joni a chance to be alone with us. Or he needed to spend some time alone with Ewan. She didn't know.

At breakfast, Mom and I barely spoke. Mom seemed preoccupied, more faraway than angry. Something was on her mind. Probably John. "What time is your train?" she asked as we cleared the breakfast dishes.

"Ten," I told her. "We better get going."

She nodded. "Are you packed?"

"Yes." I'd been packed since the night before. After our argument, I'd worked off my anger at her by jamming things into my suitcase.

"Let's go, then," she said, plucking her shoulder bag off the back of a chair.

I took my suitcase from the bottom of the stairs and joined her in the car. We pulled out of the driveway and drove for almost a mile without talking. Finally I couldn't control my curiosity anymore. I needed to know. "Are you going to break up with John this weekend?"

Without turning toward me, she nodded.

I wanted to shout, *Don't do it! A guy like John doesn't come along every day!* There didn't seem any point, though. Her mind was made up.

How would John take this news? I wished I could warn him. Maybe I'd call him when I got to the city.

As we waited on the station platform for the train, I felt I had to say *something.* "Mom, maybe you should wait," I suggested. "Think about it over the weekend."

"I can't. John wants to go out on Saturday

and I can't go on a date knowing I intend to break up with him."

I could understand that. But . . . still. "If you go on the date, maybe you'll realize that you don't want to break up."

"Stacey, John is the first man I've seriously dated since your dad and I divorced. Don't you think I should see who else is out there?"

The train arrived and cut short our conversation. Mom and John were all I could think of on the trip to the city.

Dad met me on the platform when my train pulled into Grand Central Station. I ran into his arms, so glad to see him. Even though Dad works too much, he's a great guy. He took my bag and smiled at me. "How was Thanksgiving?" he asked.

A rush of words came to mind — and stopped before they could tumble out of my mouth. Something stopped me from telling him about the Brookes. Specifically about John. It was silly, I suppose. After all, Dad had a girlfriend. Mom knew about her. Why shouldn't he know she was dating?

Although it made no sense, I couldn't do it. "Good," I said. "Quiet."

"Mine too. Samantha and I didn't feel like traveling. Too much traffic on Thanksgiving. We went to the Oak Room at the Plaza."

"Nice."

"Yes, it was," he agreed, though I sensed from his quiet voice that he'd have preferred a big family Thanksgiving.

We spent a fun day together at the Museum of Modern Art and then went to Chinatown for dinner. Afterward, we walked around the busy, narrow streets looking in shops. I bought some earrings for myself. I also bought a Chinese fan I thought Joni might like and a small ceramic dragon for Ewan. I had the feeling I might not be seeing much of them anymore. The idea made me sad.

I didn't have the chance to phone Ethan until we got back to the apartment around seven-thirty. "I'll be right over," he said.

You never saw anyone shower, wash and blow-dry her hair, and change into a new outfit so fast. In less than half an hour, Ethan was at Dad's door. And I was ready.

I have to tell you something about Ethan. He's totally adorable. He has deep blue eyes, long, almost-black hair, and a small gold ear-ring in one ear. I think he could be a model with his straight nose, high cheekbones, and wide mouth.

It might be because I don't see him often that every time I set eyes on him, I'm amazed all over again. He's the nicest guy, so easy to talk to. He's an art student here in the city. My best friend, Claudia, and my boyfriend, Ethan, are both artists. I must like artists.

"Hi, Stace," he said, wrapping me in a hug. "Happy belated Thanksgiving. How was it?"

"Wait until I tell you," I said, happy finally to be with someone I could talk things over with. Dad gave me permission to go out with Ethan as long as I was back by ten.

The air had grown very cold. I pulled up my jacket collar and jammed my hands into my pockets. We walked down Madison Avenue, looking at the people and in the stores. Ethan told me about a big art show his school was putting together. He was busy getting his work together for it. We stopped for tea in a small cafe. That was when I told him about Mom and John, and how silly Mom was acting.

Ethan leaned back in his chair. "Yeah, but she's your mom," he said. "You've got to back her up."

"Even if she's about to do something dumb?"

"She backs you up, doesn't she?" He knew she did, because I'd told him so. "She might know things about him that you don't see. He might have said stuff to her that's influencing her decision."

"Or maybe she's just afraid of getting into another relationship," I suggested.

"That could be. But it's her decision."

"I feel so bad about this," I said, "and I'm not exactly sure why."

"It might be because you and your mom had an argument," he said. "And maybe you're sorry your matchmaking didn't work."

That sounded true to me. Too true. I decided to call Mom when I returned to Dad's. That made me remember that I'd intended to call John. Oh, well, there was no sense warning him now. The deed might already have been done. Besides, I owed Mom my loyalty more than I owed it to John.

saturday

Life is strang. I wold have thot that Joni Brook would jump for joy with the way thinge are terning out. She is not tho. You better talk to her as soon as you can, Stacey.

On Saturday night Claudia showed up at the Brooke house to sit for Joni and Ewan. Unfortunately, she was the only one who still thought Mom and John had a date that night.

"You must be Claudia. Oh, wow! I'm sorry," is how John greeted her at the door.

Claudia was flustered. "Wasn't it tonight?" she asked.

"No, no, come in," he said. "It's entirely my fault. Something . . . uh . . . came up and we had to . . . change plans."

"No problem. I can go," Claudia said.

"Don't. I need to work. It's actually good that you're here. I'll introduce you to the kids. They're in the basement."

Claudia followed him downstairs. Joni was stretched out on the couch, flipping through a comic book. Ewan had built a block tower. Claudia arrived just in time to see him intentionally knock it down. "This is Claudia, kids," John told them.

They looked up glumly. "Hi," Joni grunted. Ewan gave her a wave.

"Joni and Ewan are feeling a little low tonight," John explained. "But they'll behave for you." He turned to them. "Right, kids?"

"Sure," Joni replied. Suddenly, she sat up and seemed to brighten. "Hey, I thought you weren't going out," she said. "Are you going now?"

"Sorry," he said. "I'm only working."

Joni slumped down again. "Oh."

John left, leaving Claudia there with the kids. She wasn't sure if she should ask what was wrong. I hadn't spoken to her since Thanksgiving, so she had no clue. But the fact that Mom and John weren't going out made her suspect the truth. "Anybody want to play a board game or something?" she said cheerfully.

"We have Candy Land," Ewan said.

"Want to play, Joni?" Claudia asked.

"No."

Ewan took the game from a toy chest. "She's sad because she ruined Dad's life," he explained.

"No!" Claudia cried, taken aback. "I'm sure she didn't."

"It's true," Joni told her sadly. "I did."

"I don't think that's true. What happened?"

"I was a supercreep to Mrs. McGill, so she doesn't want to see Dad anymore. She told him so last night."

"Did she say it was because of you?" Claudia asked.

"No, but I know it was. She liked him until she met me. I sent Mom away too. I was such a big pain that she couldn't take it anymore." Claudia saw that she was struggling not to cry.

"Hey," Claudia said softly, "grown-ups are weird. Don't you know that by now? They do all sorts of odd things. And it's usually not because of kids. You don't seem like a pain to me. Did your mom ever say you were a pain?"

Joni shook her head. "She wrote me a card and said she needed this time to start her career and then she'd be our mom again."

"I didn't hear the word *pain* in that. Not once," Claudia pointed out. "And you know what else? Mrs. McGill loves kids who are a pain. She loves Stacey."

"Stacey's not a pain," Ewan objected.

"Sure she is. Sometimes," said Claudia. "So am I. I'm a real pain."

"You are?" Joni asked, interested.

"Oh, yeah. I drive my parents crazy. I read Nancy Drew books, which they don't think I should waste my time on. I don't do well in school. I'm always getting paint and ink and stuff on furniture. And I eat junk food all the time, which they hate. In fact, I have some with me." She dug into the canvas bag that was still slung over her shoulder and pulled out three packs of Hostess cupcakes, one for each of them.

She also pulled out three white T-shirts and a case of fabric markers. "Hey, do you want to decorate these?" she suggested.

"Yeah," Joni said.

They went to the kitchen and spread out the T-shirts on the table. Claudia dumped the fabric pens in the middle. "Can we draw whatever we want?" Joni asked.

"Absolutely," Claudia assured her. "For the next few hours, we're in an adult-free zone."

Joni smiled and picked up a pen. "That's a relief."

"Sometimes it really is," Claudia agreed, uncapping her pen.

Joni plunged into the project with intense concentration, while Ewan sat and considered what to do for five or so minutes before marking his shirt. It wasn't long before Joni's design became clear. In the middle, a girl with brown hair and green eyes smiled as she flexed her arm muscles. A vivid yellow sun blazed above her. Below the figure Joni wrote *No Pain, No Gain.*

Claudia grinned. Something told her Joni was going to be all right.

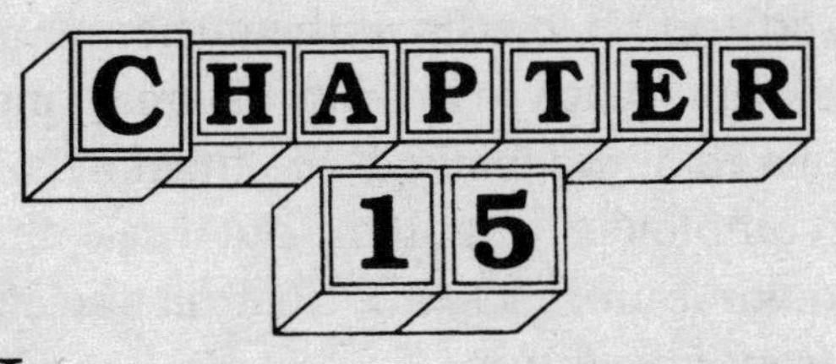

"Where were you all weekend?" I cried when Mom picked me up at the Stoneybrook train station on Sunday. "I called and called but you didn't answer. The answering machine wasn't even on." I was more relieved to see her than I was truly angry. I'd started to worry when I couldn't get in touch with her.

"John kept calling me, and after a couple of conversations I just didn't want to talk to him anymore," she explained as I slid into the car beside her.

"Isn't that a little immature?" I observed.

"Probably. But I couldn't discuss the breakup with him one more time."

"So you did it," I said. "How did it go?"

"It was fairly unpleasant. If you don't mind, I'd rather not discuss it. It's over, and that's that."

Mom didn't look happy, but if she didn't want to talk, what could I do? I remembered what Ethan had said about being supportive. I decided I needed to do what she wanted right now.

I talked about Ethan and about the exhibition Dad and I had seen at the museum.

"Are you ready for our reading group?" Mom asked as we walked into the house.

I'd completely forgotten, but I *had* finished the book. "Sure," I said. "Just let me get the book from my suitcase."

We sat together in the living room. "Mr. Darcy is really an adorable guy," I began.

"But he has his faults," Mom pointed out.

"So does Elizabeth Bennett. She's incredibly self-protective, don't you think? She's so worried about her pride and her independence that she almost loses the perfect husband."

"Maybe," Mom said. "But I thought initially you gave her credit for not doing the easy, conventional thing. It would have been so much simpler for her to be agreeable to him just because it would have been socially and economically convenient."

"You're right, I did say that," I had to admit. I'd almost forgotten. "I guess as I read further I began getting frustrated with her stubbornness. There was this great guy right in front of her and she wouldn't see it. I began to like Elizabeth a lot and I wanted her to be happy."

"Yes, but Elizabeth wanted a real marriage, a

love marriage. Nothing else would be acceptable. She wouldn't marry a man just because he was well thought of or handsome. She needed a meeting of souls. Until she found that, she couldn't accept less."

Mom's words struck me silent. Sure, they were true of *Pride and Prejudice*, but they were true of her as well.

The cordless phone on the table rang. I snapped it up. Claudia was on the other end. "Do you mind if I talk to her a minute?" I asked Mom.

"Go ahead. I want to finish the last chapter anyway."

I took the phone into the kitchen. Claudia filled me in on her sitting job. "Joni seemed a lot better by the time I left," she said. "She's still sad, though. She told me she didn't blame you if you hated her. You better talk to her."

"Thanks," I said. "I will. 'Bye."

I returned to the living room. "Mom, could we finish this later?" I said. "Claudia says Joni thinks I hate her. I'd like to go see her."

"Sure," Mom agreed. "Want a ride?"

"I'll take my bike." I was pretty sure Mom didn't want to go there, not even to the curb. I opened my suitcase and dug out the fan and the dragon. Then I put on my jacket and hopped on my bike.

John looked shocked when I turned up on

his front doorstep. "Did your mom send you?" he asked hopefully.

"Sorry. I bought some things for Joni and Ewan that I'd like to give them."

"Oh." John let me in. "In the kitchen," he said. I found them sitting at the table eating bowls of chicken noodle soup.

"Stacey!" Ewan greeted me.

"Hi, pal," I said, pulling up a chair next to Joni. "Hi, Joni."

She gave me a cautious smile. "Hi."

I handed her the fan and slid the dragon across the table to Ewan. "Cool!" he cried. "Thank you!"

"They're from Chinatown," I told the kids.

"You went to China?" Ewan cried.

"No, not exactly." I explained to him that Chinatown was a part of New York City.

"This is so beautiful," Joni said, spreading the fan in front of her. "You really bought this for me?"

"Sure I did."

"Do you know what happened?" she asked me.

I nodded. "It's not your fault, you know. My mom just isn't sure she's in love with your dad."

"You mean, it's his fault, not mine?"

"It's not even his fault. Mom thinks he's a great guy but maybe not the one for her."

"It would have been nice to be sisters," she said.

I put my hand on hers. "We still could be," I said.

"No we can't. They broke up."

"Yeah, but *we* didn't," I said. "If you ever feel that you need a big sister to talk to — call me. You too, Ewan. I could be your honorary big sister. What do you say?"

"Yea!" Ewan cried.

Joni leaned over and hugged me. Nothing could have made me happier.

So, maybe I hadn't gained a stepfamily. I now had an honorary little brother and sister. That sure was something worth having.

Dear Reader,

In *Stacey McGill . . . Matchmaker?* Stacey's personal life conflicts with her baby-sitting and puts her in a difficult position. Stacey feels caught between her troubled charges and their father, and has to decide if she can talk to Mr. Brooke without betraying the kids. Complicating matters further is the issue of Stacey's mother, who has been dating Mr. Brooke.

Baby-sitting is full of surprises. You never know what kind of situation will arise. It's important to be on your toes. Just remember that when you're responsible for younger children, safety *always* comes first. Stacey knows that her mom's feelings and her mom's relationship with Mr. Brooke are important, but when Joni storms off, Stacey realizes that Joni's safety comes first, no matter what. When you're baby-sitting, be prepared to think on your feet — and be creative!

Happy reading,

Ann M Martin

L. GODWIN

Ann M. Martin

About the Author

Ann Matthews Martin was born on August 12, 1955. She grew up in Princeton, NJ, with her parents and her younger sister, Jane.

Although Ann used to be a teacher and then an editor of children's books, she's now a full-time writer. She gets ideas for her books from many different places. Some are based on personal experiences. Others are based on childhood memories and feelings. Many are written about contemporary problems or events.

All of Ann's characters, even the members of the Baby-sitters Club, are made up. (So is Stoneybrook.) But many of her characters are based on real people. Sometimes Ann names her characters after people she knows, other times she chooses names she likes.

In addition to the Baby-sitters Club books, Ann Martin has written many other books for children. Her favorite is *Ten Kids, No Pets* because she loves big families and she loves animals. Her favorite Baby-sitters Club book is *Kristy's Big Day.* (By the way, Kristy is her favorite baby-sitter!)

Ann M. Martin now lives in New York with her cats, Gussie, Woody, and Willy. Her hobbies are reading, sewing, and needlework — especially making clothes for children.

Notebook Pages

This Baby-sitters Club book belongs to ______________________.

I am __________ years old and in the ______________________

grade.

The name of my school is ______________________________.

I got this BSC book from ______________________________.

I started reading it on ______________________________ and

finished reading it on ______________________________.

The place where I read most of this book is ________________.

My favorite part was when ______________________________.

If I could change anything in the story, it might be the part when

____.

My favorite character in the Baby-sitters Club is ____________.

The BSC member I am most like is ________________________

because ____.

If I could write a Baby-sitters Club book it would be about ____

____.

#124 Stacey McGill . . . Matchmaker?

In *Stacey McGill . . . Matchmaker?*, Stacey finds it's not easy to match people up. If I were a matchmaker, two people I would set up are ____________________ and ______________________________________. I think they would get along because ____. Two people I would *not* want to set up are ____ and ____, because ____. If a matchmaker were setting me up with someone, I would want to be set up with ____ because ____. I would *not* want to be set up with ____.

STACEY'S

Here I am, age three.

Me with Charlotte
my "almost

A family portrait — me
with my parents.

SCRAP BOOK

Johanssen, sister."

Getting ready for school.

In LUV at Shadow Lake.

Illustrations by Angelo Tillery

Read all the books
about **Stacey**
in the Baby-sitters Club series
by Ann M. Martin

#3 *The Truth About Stacey*
Stacey's different . . . and it's harder on her than anyone knows.

#8 *Boy-Crazy Stacey*
Who needs baby-sitting when there are boys around!

#13 *Good-bye Stacey, Good-bye*
How do you say good-bye to your very best friend?

#18 *Stacey's Mistake*
Stacey has never been so wrong in her life!

#28 *Welcome Back, Stacey!*
Stacey's moving again . . . back to Stoneybrook!

#35 *Stacey and the Mystery of Stoneybrook*
Stacey discovers a *haunted house* in Stoneybrook!

#43 *Stacey's Emergency*
The Baby-sitters are so worried. Something's wrong with Stacey.

#51 *Stacey's Ex-Best Friend*
Is Stacey's old friend Laine super mature or just a super snob?

#58 *Stacey's Choice*
Stacey's parents are both depending on her.
But how can she choose between them . . . again?

#65 *Stacey's Big Crush*
Stacey's in LUV . . . with her twenty-two-year-old teacher!

#70 *Stacey and the Cheerleaders*
Stacey becomes part of the "in" crowd when she tries out for the cheerleading team.

#76 *Stacey's Lie*
When Stacey tells one lie it turns to another, then another, then another . . .

#83 *Stacey vs. the BSC*
Is Stacey outgrowing the BSC?

#87 *Stacey and the Bad Girls*
With friends like these, who needs enemies?

#94 *Stacey McGill, Super Sitter*
It's a bird . . . it's a plane . . . it's a super sitter!

#99 *Stacey's Broken Heart*
Who will pick up the pieces?

#105 *Stacey the Math Whiz*
Stacey + Math = Big Excitement!

#111 *Stacey's Secret Friend*
Stacey doesn't want anyone to know that Tess is her friend.

#119 *Stacey's Ex-boyfriend*
Robert has some big problems. Can Stacey solve them?

#124 *Stacey McGill . . . Matchmaker?*
Can Stacey set up her mom with the perfect guy?

Mysteries:

#1 *Stacey and the Missing Ring*
Stacey has to find that ring — or business is over for the Baby-sitters Club!

#10 *Stacey and the Mystery Money*
Who would give Stacey counterfeit money?

#14 *Stacey and the Mystery at the Mall*
Shoplifting, burglaries — mysterious things are going on at the Washington Mall!

#18 *Stacey and the Mystery at the Empty House*
Stacey enjoys house-sitting for the Johanssens — until she thinks someone's hiding out in the house.

#22 *Stacey and the Haunted Masquerade*
This is one dance that Stacey will *never* forget!

#29 *Stacey and the Fashion Victim*
Modeling can be deadly.

#33 *Stacey and the Stolen Hearts*
Stacey has to find the thief before SMS becomes a school of broken hearts.

Portrait Collection:

Stacey's Book
An autobiography of the BSC's big city girl.

Look for #125

MARY ANNE IN THE MIDDLE

Jessi gasped and stepped back a pace. It was as if Mallory had punched her. She stared hard at Mallory, her mouth gaping.

"What?" Mallory asked. "What's the matter?"

Jessi closed her mouth and squared her shoulders. "I can't talk about this now," she said, turning away from Mallory.

"Come on, Jessi," Mallory pleaded. "Why are you so upset?"

I saw that Jessi was fighting back tears. She lunged toward the hall closet. "I have to go, Mary Anne," she said in a choked voice as she yanked her jacket from the closet. "Mallory is here now. She can help you baby-sit."

I stood up. "Come on, Jessi, don't go. Stay, and we'll talk some more."

"I can't." She fixed Mallory with an icy gaze. She no longer seemed ready to cry. Instead, she was angry again. "Besides, Mallory should probably spend some time with her brothers and sisters, since she'll be abandoning them soon."

"That is so unfair!" Mallory cried. But Jessi didn't even hear her. In the next second she was out the door.

Mallory turned toward me. "Do you believe her?" she asked.

I could only sigh deeply. I had never seen Jessi so angry.

"I thought she was my best friend," Mallory said.

"She is," I replied. I only hoped that they'd still be friends if Mallory decided to leave.